Loved at Last

Vol. 2

SALZWASSER
VERLAG

Mark Lemon

Loved at Last

Vol. 2

Reprint of the original, first published in 1864.

1st Edition 2022 | ISBN: 978-3-75259-428-7

Verlag (Publisher): Salzwasser Verlag GmbH, Zeilweg 44, 60439 Frankfurt, Deutschland
Vertretungsberechtigt (Authorized to represent): E. Roepke, Zeilweg 44, 60439 Frankfurt, Deutschland
Druck (Print): Books on Demand GmbH, In de Tarpen 42, 22848 Norderstedt, Deutschland

LOVED AT LAST.

A Story.

BY

MARK LEMON

"Not at first sight, nor with a dribbing shot,
Love gave the wound, which while I breathe will bleed:
But known worth did in tract of time proceed,
Till by degrees it had full conquest got.
I saw and liked, I liked but lovèd not;
I loved, but did not straight what love decreed."
SIR PHILIP SIDNEY.

IN THREE VOLUMES.

VOL. II.

LONDON

1864.

CONTENTS.

CHAPTER VII.

CHAPTER VIII.

CHAPTER IX.

CHAPTER X.

CHAPTER XI.

CHAPTER XII.

LOVED AT LAST.

CHAPTER I.

TREATS OF CHANGES PAST AND TO COME.—MR. HARTLEY PROPOSES TO RESUME RELATIONS WITH MRS. MASHAM.—THE FACE SEEN BY THE FIRE-LIGHT.

THE hunting days of Mr. Lockyer were nearly over. The love of the chase is an enduring passion, and rarely leaves those who have encouraged it from their youth upward, no, not when age and infirmity forbid a further indulgence in its delightful excitements. The old sportsman even then finds other 'happy hunting-grounds' if an old crony, seated snugly by a sea-coal fire, recounts the moving incidents and accidents by flood and field, and, better still, when mounted on Old Memory if he himself be permitted to cheer on the hounds and lead the field. Mr. Lockyer's sporting friends were unfortunately rather limited in number both in town and country, and his home at Holly Lodge would have been rarely enlivened by such pleasant recitals as we have indicated, had he not usually driven in his small pony carriage to those meets which were within reach from his house, and thereby obtained a look at the hounds and a brief gossip with some sympathising sportsman, who not unfrequently was induced to accept an invitation to lunch should circumstances permit, or make one at the family dinner.

As his compulsory relaxation from business did not produce any salutary effects on Mr. Lockyer's health, it was determined to admit Frank as a junior partner into his father's firm, and arrangements for that purpose were accordingly made. Mr. Lockyer was not a very wealthy man, as he had sustained some very considerable losses by the Jamaica connections of the house, and it became incumbent upon Frank to give a closer application to business than he had hitherto done. His visits therefore to Holly Lodge were less frequent and of shorter duration than they had hitherto been; but he generally contrived to find time to call at the Rosebush to present Ruth with some musical novelty, and afford her the benefit of his own more cultivated taste in giving effect to the composition. Frank had established such excellent relations with Mrs. Masham that the watchful mother intruded herself only at intervals upon the young people, and their conversations consequently assumed the freedom of a *tête-à-tête,* neither suspecting the danger of their pleasant intercourse, or perceiving the influence it was to have upon their after lives. Miss Wycherly was occasionally of the party, when visiting her friend and *protégée;* and then Frank Lockyer displayed his lady-killing powers to the utmost, usually returning from the Rosebush self-satisfied, if not altogether happy. Frank occasionally made calls at Old Court, and would have gladly accepted any encouragement to have repeated them more frequently; but for some unexplained reason he always left Miss Wycherly with the uncomfortable feelings of a man who had been made conscious that his most agreeable sayings had gone for nothing, and who had been, in short, rather snubbed than encouraged to persevere in his complimentary visitations.

The Wycherlys, however, left Old Court (occasionally also) on a rambling holiday in France and Belgium, and then Ruth had the monopoly of his agreeableness and attention.

During these short and pleasant meetings the absent Cecil was never forgotten, and Frank repeated or read such portions of the letters which he had received from his friend as he thought were calculated to amuse, until he fancied that the proper recognition of his own claims to consideration was somewhat lessened by the interest displayed in Cecil. Why should he have been thus sensitive, trifler that he was? He had asked himself that question, and smiled at his own weakness. Nevertheless he could not help resenting this favoured preference, and said one day when Cecil had been mentioned more than once:—

"I shall be writing to the old boy when I go back to town, and shall not fail to tell him how interested you are about him. I declare, Ruth"—he had come to call her Ruth—"I declare I am growing jealous of Master Cecil."

These words were idly spoken, but they brought a blush to Ruth's pretty face, and silence to her tongue.

Frank, with all his self-conceit, was a warm, true-hearted friend, and believing that he had offended Ruth by some implied detraction of Cecil, he reproached himself for uttering what might have seemed to her an ungenerous remark, and said:

"He is a dear, noble fellow, and deserves to be loved and remembered at all times. I miss him sadly, and shall do so until he returns."

"And when may that be?" asked Ruth quietly.

"Not until the end of the year, I am afraid. He has some difficult business to manage, but he writes hopefully about it. When he comes back, Ruth, I shall bring him down to Holly Lodge and make a whole week's holiday. You will be glad of that, shall you not?" As he asked this he looked at her so kindly, so tenderly, that the blush returned again, and though her lips moved, no sound came from them. "I am sure you will," said Frank, guessing at her answer, "and we will try and make the time pass as happily as it did when we first met; I mean when we were all together at this jolly old Rosebush. Miss Wycherly will have returned, you know, and perhaps her good prejudiced papa will take more kindly to Cecil, now that he and his father are separated."

"I have no doubt but Mr. Wycherly will be more just to cousin Cecil, for my mother has used all her influence to remove the unfavourable impression created by his connection with Mr. Hartley. Poor Cecil! how dearly his mother loves him," said Ruth.

"Yes," replied Frank, rather seriously. "It is impossible for any one to know him thoroughly and not love him. I wish I were half as good a fellow."

Ruth looked into Frank's face with her full bright eyes, and if he could have read their meaning, and the meaning also of the faint smile which played around her lips, he might have learned the secret of a maiden's heart, and have startled Cecil by the discovery.

But Frank, the clever, agreeable lady-killer, was a dullard, and had never made a study of woman's heart: her prettiness and outward graces had hitherto contented him. He little thought how learned he was to become in that loving and enduring mystery.

There were changes coming when least expected, and the Rosebush was destined to own another mistress than Mrs. Masham. The little school-room of Professor Ruth was soon to be deprived of its small *alumni*, and become degraded to a dry skittle-ground; the sanctum even, once the abode of love,—for woman's friendship is love, with his pinions grown,—and wherein the heiress of Old Court and her pupil Ruth had held sweet maiden converse, or evoked eloquent music from the modest piano standing in the corner, whereby the light could fall upon the music page, and leave the minstrel's blush or pallor unseen by the attendant cavalier who sang so feelingly of love, perchance. This sanctum even was soon to be devoted to the rude orgies of bucolic revellers, scaring away the pretty loves and graces which had nestled about it for five long years or more, and ever since Ruth and her mother and her friends had met within it. Frank Lockyer received his first intimation of the change which was coming from an auctioneer's large posting-bill affixed on either side of the doorway of the Rosebush Inn, announcing that all sorts of goods and chattels pertaining to the hostelry would "be sold without reserve, unless disposed of by private contract before the day announced for sale."

Frank read the announcement with much surprise and anxiety, as he foreboded that a blight had come upon the Rosebush. He knew how often those announcements of the rude dispersion of goods and chattels were like marks upon plague-stricken houses, and told what hopes were lying dead within; and he remembered that Mrs. Masham had had her bitter experiences of a broken home. He was much relieved therefore when Mrs. Masham smiled as she received him, although she was attired in slight mourning. Moreover he knew that she had taken such constant pride in her little inn, that one would have thought she must have loved it, as people have been known to have surrounded their hearts with bricks and timber, and when they have been dragged forth from them by hard and cruel fortune, have pined away in distant lands. But Mrs. Masham stood in her doorway between the loud announcement of the prospective abandonment of her home, and smiled a welcome to Mr. Frank Lockyer, who read the bills again with wondering eyes. And yet he could not discover the story connected with the announcement. As several persons with whom we have made acquaintance are interested in the changes which are taking place, we shall hear what Mr. Hartley may have to say upon the subject.

Whatever anxiety might have lodgement in the bosom of Mr. Hartley, he never allowed it to interfere with the progress of his dinner, and he rarely permitted himself any other conversation during that meal than occasional comments on its components, generally in disparagement of the cook or of his wedded housekeeper. He had been more than usually silent one day, being only provoked into very vehement speech by discovering a raisin-stone in his pudding. He then continued to jerk out rude observations to his wife, until the production of his private Stilton somewhat allayed his irritation.

The cloth had been removed and Mr. Hartley

had drunk his second glass of sherry before he spoke again.

"I suppose, Rebecca," he said, "you write to those people at Hilltown now and then—the Mashams I mean?"

"Write!" replied Mrs. Hartley, astonished at the question, as no reference was ever made to the persons just mentioned.

"Yes, w-ri-te!" said Hartley impatiently. "Correspond, I suppose you call it. You do, I suppose?"

"Indeed I do not. You forbade me," said Mrs. Hartley.

"O yes!—that's a reason, ain't it? Well, if you haven't, you ought to have done. Women always do as they're told when they oughtn't, and *vice versâ*; there certainly is a twist in the female character that wants taking out," remarked Hartley.

"I never disobey you, Selwyn," said his wife.

"Don't you? Didn't you go to Hilltown when I said don't?" replied Hartley.

"I went to do a mother's duty," said Mrs. Hartley; "to be with our son——"

"And a pretty grateful return he has made us," replied Hartley, as usual interrupting his wife. "I don't know why I have a fatherly—a fatherly what's-its-name for him, after his conduct to me, and if you'd looked after his interests a little more, and indulged him less, it would have been better for all of us. Well, that's past mending; but if I'd lived in anybody's house as long as you did at that Hollybush—no, Rosebush place, I'd have known what money they had, and what their expectations were, if they had any."

"I really don't understand you, Selwyn."

"I dare say not. I didn't marry you for what was inside your head, but for what was outside of it once upon a time," said Hartley. "Well, that's past mending also. Now I tell you what; you must write down there on some excuse or other. Cecil left an old pair of boots, didn't he? or if he didn't, you can ask the question as an ice-breaker."

Mrs. Hartley was confounded, and could not reply for some moments.

"Are you serious—I mean—for what purpose am I to do this?"

"If I say to please me, I suppose you'll say you won't do it, and therefore I'll be open at once with you," said Hartley. "It's to serve that ungrateful son of yours, Cecil."

"How, Selwyn?" asked Mrs. Hartley.

"How? If you'd have made use of your opportunities, there would have been no trouble in the matter; but as you go about with your head under your wing like an old hen a-roosting, perhaps we've lost the chance of making Cecil independent."

Mrs. Hartley could but look patiently, and wait for an explanation of her tyrant's meaning.

"Did you ever hear of Philip Masham?" asked Hartley, after a pause.

"Yes; he went to India, I have heard you say."

"Yes, to India," continued Hartley, pausing

again. "He was Uncle Selwyn's residuary legatee, if you know what that means. He came in for a good slice of the property which they made such a row about."

Mrs. Hartley grew very pale, expecting some further disgraceful disclosures.

"Wycherly looked precious sharp after that, an old scamp," muttered Hartley.

"Philip was entitled to what he received, was he not?" asked Mrs. Hartley, hardly knowing what she said.

"Yes; no one disputed that," and Hartley drained the decanter into his glass and drank off the wine.

"Why did they dispute the other legacies?" said Mrs. Hartley, as though she were impelled to make the inquiry.

Hartley dashed the empty glass upon the table, shivering it into fragments.

"Who told you they disputed it, madam? Who told you that? I never did; but you've been listening to the slandering lies of those people at Hilltown, and I've seen it—known it, ever since you came back from the place."

"Selwyn!" Mrs. Hartley could say no more, but sat silent and alarmed.

"I say that the will was a true will, and I took under it only what I had a right to. I am not going to sit at my own table and be told otherwise, and by my own wife."

Hartley rose and paced about the room for some moments. When Mrs. Hartley could recover herself sufficiently to speak, she said:—

"Selwyn, I have never said one unwifely word to you in all my life. I have never accused you of any wrong, and if, as you seem to imply, others have done so, why have you asked me to resume an acquaintance which has ceased at your request?"

"I'll tell you presently," said Hartley, sitting down, pursing his lips together, and thrusting his hands into his pockets, adding, after a pause, "I'll tell you why I was so put out if you'll leave off snivelling; I can never speak to you now but what you begin that game. Well, have you done?"

Mrs. Hartley wiped away the tears which had come unbidden.

"There have been a great many unpleasant things said about my uncle's will, but they were lies, as I could have proved had they gone to trial. Old Susan could have proved 'em so; that Jim Perks that used to come here could have proved also. Very well. Now, when years have gone by and all old scores ought to be forgotten, that Philip Masham, who got more than he ever expected to get, must bring up the old lies again and put 'em into writing."

Mrs. Hartley uttered a faint cry, and with terror in her face and eyes looked steadfastly at her husband.

"Don't look at me in that way," said Hartley, "as though you didn't believe they were lies—made up to cheat me of what was my own,—of what I had earned dearly enough by—by years of services for which I charged nothing. Uncle knew that, and paid me in his will. Do you believe that?"

"Yes, I will believe that," replied Mrs. Hartley.

"Well, do, and teach Master Cecil to do the same," said Hartley, wiping his forehead with his hand. "And now let us talk calmly, if we can. My manager, Mr. Bosbury, has a brother who is clerk in a lawyer's office. They're correspondents to some concern in India, and they've just received the copy of Philip Masham's will."

"Is he dead then?"

"Of course he is, or how could he have made his will?—well, I mean what would be the use of his will? Now, seeing my name mentioned in it, he—that's the clerk—very properly tells his brother, who—very properly too—tells the other to make a rough copy of it, which he does. Now this Philip Masham had talked of coming over here for the last ten years and settling; but, like a good many others, he could not leave off making money until he had lost his liver.

He dies and settles for good in India, leaving a widow—a native woman—behind him. They used to burn themselves once on a time, which saved a good deal of trouble in the way of settlement. That's done away with—by the Humane Society I believe. Here, let's have another half pint of sherry."

Mrs. Hartley rose and obeyed the mandate. Whilst she was doing so, Hartley opened his great pocket-book and produced a paper. Having taken some of the wine, he spoke on.

"Here are the heads of Master Philip's precious will. Do you mind hearing what he says about me?"

Mrs. Hartley shook her head to prevent him reading anything that would be painful for her to hear; but he, judging by his own callous nature, interpreted the action otherwise.

"Oh, you don't," he said; "I am sure I don't mind reading it. It's not in law jargon, as it isn't a copy, only a summary—heads like. He says, 'that in consequence of the unjust treatment my brother experienced at the hands of Jacob Hartley—' I believe," said Hartley, pausing in the reading, "I could upset Philip's will on that statement, and leaving out the 'Selwyn;' but it ain't worth my while to do it. Well: 'treatment of Jacob Hartley, I bequeath to my niece, Ruth Masham, so many rupees'—ever so many—'as will bring her in three hundred a year sterling, and at my wife's death the residue of my property in India.'—There's luck for your friend at the Beggar's Bush!—'Also, I bequeath to my sister-in-law, Mrs. Hester Masham, an annuity of two hundred a year.' In case of death *et cetera*, that goes to Ruth. What do you think of that, ma'am?"

"I am delighted to hear it," said Mrs. Hartley, looking the pleasure she felt.

"I should like to know why? We shan't be a shilling the richer. I get all the kicks and they get all the ha'pence; but, as I said before, there's a twist in the female mind that always makes it see things in wrong lights. Now, having read all that to you, do you understand now why I want you to open up a correspondence with those people down there?"

"I confess I do not, Selwyn," replied Mrs. Hartley.

"And yet you pretend to be always thinking of your children, dead or alive, ma'am. Don't you see the chance that Cecil has lost by your not finding out the expectations which these people had from Philip Masham?" asked Hartley.

"I never heard them mention his name," replied Mrs. Hartley.

"I dare say not; they were too deep for that; but if you'd pumped them about their affairs you'd have got at it; and then, if Cecil hadn't been a downright fool, he would have stuck up to this Ruth and married her. It may be too late now, as he won't be back for these three months, I expect; and somebody else may hang up his hat at Mrs. Masham's."

Mrs. Hartley knew not what to say. She had no arguments to which her husband would listen to offer in opposition to this teaching, and therefore she remained silent.

"Well," said Hartley, after a while, "let what has passed fructify till morning, and then, if you can't see your way to writing, I'll draw you up a letter, or get Mr. Jones, my chief clerk, to do it; he's the best gammoner I ever knew. The number of scrapes—I mean little difficulties—that he has written us out of nobody can tell: I can't. Clever fellow! A genius, I should say, if that was a respectable word to use of a man with his commercial qualifications. He's a treasure, and only a hundred-and-fifty a year, with tea on the premises. Good-night, my dear!"

When he had left the room Mrs. Hartley rested her head between her hands and gazed fixedly upon the table, until she saw pictures of the past and of the present come and vanish, sometimes distinct and separate,—sometimes confused and mingling together. Bright scenes were few indeed, and those ever giving place to dark and painful imagery—the present darkest of all.

And then she wondered why her married life should have been so full of sorrow—wondered, until she remembered that she had wedded without loving, lured to the altar by a silly vanity, which had told her that she had a pretty face and a lithe form, which he who had praised them so often would never tire of praising. The home she had left had been poorly furnished, scantily supplied with physical comfort, but there had always been present a mother's love to watch for her wants and to minister even to her fancies. The home she came to gradually increased in evidences of wealth and plenty, but no love, no tender solicitude from him who had sworn at God's altar that they should be a portion of her married life. Her children,—yes, they had brought with them their dowries of love, and did not take them back again when they themselves returned to heaven; but even the precious blessings which they bestowed lost in part their comfort, knowing how little they were valued by her unfeeling husband. The future!—she dared not seek to look into the future; but, covering her face, though there were none to be witnesses of her tears, wept bitterly.

Cecil was away. At times she rejoiced to know that he was free from his father's influence—secured from a knowledge of his father's meanness and tricky plans: she was compelled so to characterise the confidences he had made; and then her poor weary heart yearned towards her son, believing that it could find a resting-place if he were near her. Poor wife! poor mother!

There was news of Cecil in a day or two, and his long, loving letter brought comfort to the one who needed it so much.

Frank Lockyer had a letter also, and a part of it must find a place in our story. In a former letter Cecil had written:—

"I have had an adventure coming out which reads something like romance, but it is quite true. You will remember no doubt our ride through Pemberton Wood, when I saw the poacher's face distinctly shown by the flash of his gun-pan. I told you I could recognise that face again, see it where I might. One evening I was walking the deck and looking into the galley (where they cook), I saw by the light of the fire the very face I had seen in Pemberton Wood. I was so satisfied of the correctness of my recollection that I spoke to the man and found that I was right. He had been a poacher, and was out that night, proving to be no other than the Jim Perks who made that painful revelation to my mother: you shall know more of that some day, perhaps. Well, I found that the poor fellow had been allowed to drift down, even into a gaol; but by my mother's help and that of Miss Wycherly he had been enabled to emigrate. There—odd, was it not? We had many talks together on board ship, and Miss Wycherly seems to have been his guardian angel. He was never tired of talking of her goodness, nor was I tired of listening; though why I should find such deep interest in what relates to that young lady I cannot guess."

"But I can," thought Frank; and he felt a momentary anger aroused by his conclusion. "You're half in love with her, old boy, as every one else seems to be, notwithstanding her evident pride and singular coldness. I seem to be as much a stranger to her after six months' intimacy as I was the day we met at Old Court." Yes, the lady-killer was angry with some one.

The letter which Frank had received later, and to which we have referred, said this :—

"I was back in New York yesterday, and found my poaching friend, Jim Perks, steadily at work as a porter in a commission store. He is well placed, but perfectly miserable. The fellow ought to have been born a Swiss, for he has the *maladie de pays* so strongly that he positively pines for the old country. It is ludicrous enough, but somehow I have found myself taking the trouble to argue him into sense. Not the least use, and so out of regard for his veneration (there is no other word) for you know who"—of course he could guess—"I have half-promised Perks that when I come home and get settled I will try to give him employment with me."

Frank called Cecil an "old donkey" and some other names of affectionate opprobrium; but then Frank could not lift the veil which shrouds the future, often hiding from human ken the knowledge which would rob life of all its sweetness.

Frank was not altogether pleased with Cecil's letter. It made him thoughtful at intervals throughout the day, and he once nearly wrote in his ledger "Miss Wycherly," instead of Waghorn and Company. What right had he to be thinking of the heiress of Old Court, when he had left gentle Ruth only on the yesterday, after a pleasant hour's chat, wherein he had learned that Mrs. Masham was retiring from business on the annuity which Uncle Philip had left her so considerately?

Frank is a trifler, and, like the moth—well, there is no better simile than the old, very old moth and the candle—and Frank may singe his wings at last.

CHAPTER II.

CECIL RETURNS FROM AMERICA, AND MAKES SOME PAINFUL DISCOVERIES AT HOME AND ABROAD.

THE prologue—to speak according to the fashion of the day—of Frank Lockyer's life had been played out. A youth exempt from any troubles that could have been called cares, although with a reckless hand he had sown, broadcast as it wére, wheat and tares, flowers and thistles, as he would find when the harvest-time had come. When the curtain rises again he has a widowed mother to comfort and care for, and an increase of the graver duties which he had undertaken. Apart from these changes, he had still a bright future seemingly before him, and there was small alloy mixed with the golden present.

The Wycherlys had made a longer stay upon the Continent than they had first proposed, and the autumn was well advanced when they returned to England. Frank was agreeably surprised one day to find that Wycherly had called at his place of business and left a note inviting him to visit his friends from Old Court when he should be passing their lodgings at No. 755 in the Strand. They dined at six, and should be glad to see him *sans cérémonie.*

Frank could not account for the pleasure which this invitation gave him, and he discovered instantly that he had business at Charing Cross: he wanted some cigars from Pontet's, and would take the Wycherlys in his way, the more especially as the day was rainy; and the streets of London when coated with black mud, are not tempting for out-door amusement, even to country cousins.

Mr. Lockyer therefore made rapid progress with his correspondence and other business requiring his personal attendance, postponing a few not very pressing matters until the next day, and when he had made the most of his personal advantages, proceeded in a cab to No. 755 in the Strand.

Miss Wycherly was at home, and received Mr. Lockyer with such evident pleasure that her visitor for a moment or two remained unconscious of the presence of Mrs. Masham and her daughter Ruth. So great or gratifying was his surprise on discovering his friends of the Rosebush, that it suffocated an elegant compliment which he had manufactured on his way from the City for the acceptance of Miss Kate. His confusion in consequence was quite charming—we believe that is the phrase,—but the party were soon at their ease, chatting away, Frank utterly regardless of the cabman outside, and who was reckoning every ten minutes as a quarter of an hour in the calculation of his prospective fare, a favourite mode of indemnification for loss of time with London cabmen on a wet and every other day.

The Mashams had come to town on business, and were lodging close at hand, which was very delightful. They were staying dinner; and as Mr. Wycherly had left his commands that Mr. Lockyer was to be invited to stay also, should he favour them with a call, Mr. Frank, with a slight apology for his morning *toilette*, promised to return when he had transacted the very important business he had in charge—at Pontet's.

A cheerful, simple dinner, and a very pleasant evening afterwards. Ruth and Kate singing, and Frank also, during those intervals when Mr. Wycherly ceased repeating his hand-book of Paris to him and Mrs. Masham.

It was nearly eleven before Frank left his country friends, and as the rain had ceased, he resolved to walk home to his mother's villa at Putney. He mused as he went, and thought he had never known Kate so unreserved and agreeable; for hitherto she had always become silent whenever he had attempted to interest her in a conversation. But to-night she had encouraged him to talk with her, and appeared to receive him really as a friend. The absence of restraint was due to her recent experiences of society, or perhaps—well, the lady-killer indulged in other conjectures. As for Ruth, he thought she had never looked so pretty or so graceful, and one or two remarks which she had made had pleased him by the good sense which they displayed. Dress had done something for her, and perhaps the consciousness that she was now more upon an equality with her friends had given her confidence in herself; but she certainly had never appeared so deserving of the love and admiration which Miss Wycherly had always entertained for her. "Full many a gem," &c., he repeated, and thought that Ruth might have "blushed unseen" but for the accident of her new fortunes and her acquaintance with a certain lady and gentleman who had invaded her retreat under the shadow of the Rosebush.

And Cecil had never been mentioned during the whole evening! Yes—once by Aunt Hester, and before the return of Mr. Wycherly. That was rather singular, he thought, for when he and Ruth had last talked together, he remembered to have been a little piqued at the frequency of her inquiries concerning her cousin. He would have wondered more at the omission of Cecil's name from the past evening's conversation had he known that all that he had told Ruth of his absent friend had been written down next day in a certain purple-covered diary, secured from prying eyes by a gilt lock, of which Ruth kept the key hidden in her bosom. And so Frank went to bed and dreamed that he was pulling up to Henley against tide, and getting into all kinds of difficulties with barges and lock-keepers, never once recalling Kate or Ruth in his vision, as he had hoped to have done.

The next morning Ruth rose early and busied herself until her mother came down to breakfast, writing in her purple diary, and then, when released from duty at the table, seating herself at the window which looked out upon the street, while her mother read the morning paper.

Ruth had never been in London before, and all

that she had read and heard of the great city had in no way prepared her for the impressions which it had created. At first she was almost bewildered by its vastness, seeing, whichever way she looked, streets as populous as all Hilltown. The great, grand buildings surrounding her on every side made the Elizabethan Hospital in the old town a dwarfed pile of dirty brickwork. The countless carriages of all kinds, passing to and from the busy Strand, set her wondering at the wealth of a community which could employ them, and the never-ceasing troops of passers-by made her recollections of poor little Hilltown's market-place appear reminiscences of a desert. And then she thought how all this life which she looked out upon had been preceded for hundreds of years by other living men and women who had passed away into the great beyond, and that long before another year had sped many that she now saw in health and strength would have followed to dusky death, and in how brief a space of time all would have given place to a new generation, by whom the present would be forgotten as though it had never been.

Whilst these highly original thoughts possessed her, the girl's face suddenly grew rosy red, and her lips, parted by a smile, disclosed her pearly teeth as she waved her handkerchief up and down, and nodded her pretty head in unison. It was a commonplace incident enough which had produced this sudden demonstration. Mr. Frank Lockyer was passing on his way to business, seated on the knifeboard of a Fulham omnibus! When he had passed, Ruth, without disturbing her mother by a word, took up her purple diary and retreated to her own room. She closed the door, and no one had a right to enter.

Mr. Wycherly had paid flying visits to Old Court since his return from the Continent; but the approaching harvest made it necessary for the agriculturist to leave London. At the earnest entreaties of Ruth and Mrs. Masham, Kate was permitted to remain behind as "it would give them so much pleasure to have Kate for their first guest, now that they had the power to entertain her." Mr. Wycherly could not resist such an appeal to his consideration, and as he would have much business to occupy him at Old Court, he consented to manage without the light of his home for a fortnight—well, three weeks, if he found he *could* do without her.

Mr. Frank Lockyer swore fealty to the ladies forthwith, and carried his two queens of beauty and their *chaperone* to all the gay tournaments then accessible; but when the trees begin to wear their sere and yellow leaves in the country, the flowers of the fashionable season in London have become sadly faded also; and people more acclimatised to the great metropolis than Frank's friends would have been less satisfied with the amusements selected for them. Mr. Wycherly was very fond of music (so he said, although he had been accused of falling asleep during the performance of an oratorio), but cared little for the acted drama, detesting hot theatres and late hours. As the ladies therefore had been content to consult his taste solely, and as yet had not visited a theatre, Mr. Frank was to have the honour of conducting them to a private box at one of the most popular of the London houses. Years ago, Mrs. Masham had gone the round with poor dear Peter, but Ruth and Kate had to make their first acquaintance with the fascinations of the stage.

How many remember, when graver and brighter occurrences are forgotten, their first introduction to that world of shadows. Sometimes remembered as a voyage to Elf-land, when all the tales told by a mother's voice of wondrous bean-stalks reaching to the clouds; of fairy godmothers who change pumpkins into gilded coaches, and rats and mice and such small gear into prancing steeds and powdered lacqueys; and legends of raw-headed giants and valiant giant-killers were proved to be realities, and not the fables of nursery story-books. Sometimes as the first insight into the naughty world, where wickedness walks about wearing the mask of virtue, until time detects the cheat and brings a righteous punishment. Sometimes, as our first experience, that love is a pleasant pain allied to many sorrows which purify it when true, making it the greatest blessing man can know. And sometimes it is remembered as a peep into the sibyl's glass, wherein we saw the foreshadowing of our future fate, and knew it not.

But we are keeping Mr. Lockyer's party in the lobby.

The play or drama, or whatever was the generic name of the piece represented, was not one of any poetic pretensions, and set forth only some time-honoured situations and display of emotions, loving youth and crabbed age, cunning roguery and simple virtue, and all made happy at last except the wicked. Ruth and Kate, entranced by what they saw and heard, sat, each clasping a hand of the other, when the happiness of the lovers was imperilled, and smiling at each other when the lovers obtained the advantage. They trembled when roguery seemed about to crush virtue, and relieved their pent-up sympathy with deep sighs when the innocent victim brought the wicked man to a bad end. And so the play, Frank thought, was over until the curtain should rise on another night to a different audience; but to one of those young maiden hearts it was to be acted again and again for many a day and night to come, he playing the lover's part and winning the truest love that ever possessed the soul of woman. Why?

Why! Had he not selected this show of human life, knowing its fable, and what the actors in it were to say and suffer and gain? He had so said more than once; and woe to her if she in her weakness had misunderstood the meaning of his words, associating them as she had done with all that had gone before.

It was well that Cecil Hartley returned from America a fortnight sooner than had been expected. Frank found him waiting his friend's arrival at his office in the City. Their greeting of each other was such as may be imagined to have taken plaoe between two friends so sincerely attached.

Little more remains to be told of Cecil's proceedings than is already known. He had been successful in recovering all the money due to Mr. Philcher, and had thus earned the means to commence a life of independence. He had discovered moreover that it was owing to the debtor's honesty, and not to any cleverness on the part of Mr. Philcher or any one else, that the old claim had been recognised. A quick run of success had enabled the emigrant trader to make payment of former obligations, and he would have done so at an earlier date but for the oppressive exactions of Philcher and Co. Mr. Hartley never confessed to his late partner, nor to his own son, the means by which he had obtained the information of the absent debtor's capacity and willingness to clear off old scores.

Not he—he was too sharp for that.

"When did you arrive in London?" asked

Frank. "We did not expect you until the next packet."

"I came from Liverpool yesterday," said Cecil, "having written to my mother to tell her of my return to England. Before going home to Suburban Square I called upon my father here in the City, and such a welcome as he gave me! I might have been one of his 'job lots' from the commercial and only commercial interest he appeared to feel on my safe arrival."

"You are used to his parental indifference, or should be, Cecil, and ought not to distress yourself as you evidently do," replied Frank, laying his hand on his friend's shoulder and giving him a gentle shake.

"I wish I could forget that he is my father," said Cecil; "but I was thinking then of the marked change I observed in my poor mother. He is killing her as surely as though he fed her with poison. If I can only make a home for her, if I can but secure the probability of a moderate income, I will take her from the misery of her wretched home."

"You must be prudent, for her sake as well as your own, Cecil. You must not show your teeth until you dare to bite," said Frank, gravely. "Get your present business with your father arranged, keep him to his promise of payment for your recent services, and then have no fear for the future."

Cecil compressed his lips together until they became bloodless before he spoke again. He then said :—

"Frank, I must tell you what I heard last night, though it be to expose more meanness of my father. I could see by my mother's manner that something had passed during my absence, something wherein I was concerned, that distressed her; but which, with her usual patient endurance, she was trying to bear in silence. When my father left us at night he said, in his sneering manner, 'Now you have got him back, you had better ask his permission to do your duty as my wife. He's not the fool you take him for, I'll bet an even five shillings,' and then he left the room. It was long before I could bring my mother to explain what he meant, and then she told me that he had almost used violence because she had refused, until my return, to invite correspondence with the Mashams, in order that I might propose to Ruth, who had been left——"

"That trouble is ended then, old boy," said Frank, interrupting him, seeing how much Cecil was distressing himself. "Aunt and cousin are in London, and I am their cavalier, and shall introduce you as soon as you please. So your mother is spared the mortification of writing anything."

Frank then told Cecil all that had occurred lately, and how (now that Mr. Wycherly had gone home) not an interview passed without some kindly mention of Cousin Cecil, and how anxious Aunt Hester and Ruth were for his return.

"And why should you not visit them?" asked Frank.

"I know of no reason," replied Cecil, with a smile, "as I have no design upon Ruth's heart or pocket; for, rather than pursue my father's plan for enriching myself, I would buy the good-will of the black man's crossing at Waithman's corner, and depend upon London mud for my daily bread. It would be cleaner than any he could offer me."

"Quite true, old boy," said Frank; "and as soon as I have attended to a few matters of business we will call on the Mashams, who will be delighted to see you. By-the-by, I did not tell you that Miss Wycherly is visiting them, did I?"

"Miss Wycherly?" replied Cecil, the blood from his heart deepening the bronze of his face. "No, you did not mention that she was staying there, and perhaps—perhaps I ought not to intrude upon——"

"By George!" said Frank, laughing heartily, "I do believe you are afraid of that country beauty. Well, not beauty—though she is proud enough to be one. I beg pardon," he added, seeing that Cecil was looking very grave, "I forgot that you had been touched in that quarter, and perhaps have found favour in the bright dark eyes of my Lady Basilisk in return."

"I have no such pretension, old fellow," replied Cecil. "I certainly admire Miss Wycherly, as who does not?—but I boast of no conquest. You are the lady-killer, remember."

"Lady-killer!" said Frank, impatiently. "I hate the name of Lady-killer; and as far as Kate Wycherly is concerned, I am perfectly powerless. If I smile at her, she cuts me down with a frown; if I venture to approach her with the most commonplace compliment, she pins me through with some pertness to which I dare not make a rejoinder. I not only forgive her for your sake, Cecil—don't blush, my man—but will try to love my enemy, if you'll permit me."

"Have your joke, Frank," replied Cecil, "I'm content to be your butt—too glad to hear your old voice again. I will go with you when you are at leisure."

It was then arranged between the two friends that they should call on the Mashams in the afternoon, and as soon as Frank had discharged his necessary duties in the City, they took their way to the Strand.

The Mashams and Kate were at home, and Frank having preceded Cecil into the room, said :—

"I have ventured to bring a stranger with me, but one I am half inclined to think may not be unwelcome—Mr. Cecil Hartley."

Ruth instantly rose and hastened to the door, holding out both her hands to Cecil, and then led him to her mother; who, after a moment's hesitation, kissed the bronzed cheek of the unexpected visitor.

The face of Kate Wycherly reddened and her eyelids closed as Cecil advanced to greet her, and her bosom rose and fell so rapidly that she could with difficulty speak the briefest words of welcome.

Why?

Could she be so unjust, so cruel as to connect Cecil with his father's evil life, and have permitted Mr. Wycherly's long-cherished contempt—almost detestation—of Selwyn Hartley to have begot in her mind a similar feeling? There came a cloud upon her face, red and angry, foreboding a coming storm. Some strife was in her bosom, some contest of will or passion, hatred or love, and which the brave girl strove to bear without betraying her victory or defeat.

Ruth fortunately came to her friend's rescue with some kind questions as to Mrs. Hartley's surprise and pleasure at Cecil's shortened stay in America; and Cecil, embarrassed by what he saw, could with difficulty make answer—more to his own surprise than to that of quick-sighted Ruth. Mrs. Masham then took up the conversation, and being led into a narration of her own new fortunes, contintued to talk for some time without requiring any particular assistance from Cecil to maintain the conversation. Before she had quite finished, Ruth and Kate suddenly left the room, the former returning very shortly to say that Miss Wycherly had been complaining of indisposition during the morning, and was now compelled to keep her chamber. All this was natural enough, and ought to have provoked no particular comment, but Cecil saw in it a hidden meaning which sent a pang through his heart, and made him impatient to get away.

When he and Frank had reached the street, he walked on silently for some time, scarcely regarding the first few observations of his friend, until Frank said :—

"Don't you think Ruth marvellously improved since the old days at the Rosebush?"

"Yes," replied Cecil, "certainly. She has more manner, more self-possession. She seems to have found that she has a place in the world, and has resolved to maintain it."

"She is prettier too, I fancy," said Frank. "She was almost too gentle, I used to think. And Kate Wycherly—her continental run has brought her out wonderfully; though, by-the-by, you have had but little opportunity of judging."

"Pardon me, Frank—I have, of one side of her character," replied Cecil gravely. "She has a full share of her father's prejudice, and his inconsiderateness in showing it."

"What do you mean?"

"She has not forgotten whose son I am, and though I have never offended her by word or deed, tells me plainly that I shall not intrude myself upon her, although she must have seen how bitterly I suffer from my inseparable connection with my father. But I forgive her."

"My old boy, you are too sensitive," said Frank, pressing his friend's arm. "She could not be so unjust, so unfeeling. I know her a great deal better than you do. She looked ill when we entered, and the next time you meet, you will find her as kind as she ought to be."

"Possibly," replied Cecil, "but I shall not put her to the test for some time to come, if I can help it. She has many noble qualities, I am certain—her constant friendship for poor Ruth—not poor now it seems—her devotion to her father among them; and that man will be a happy one who wins her love."

Frank thought so too, and said "Yes."

"I had heard so much of her from that man, Perks, that I seemed to have known her from her childhood, and I confess, her marked rejection of my friendship stung me to the quick. However, such experiences are part of my inheritance, and I must school myself to bear with them."

"A stupid want of self-appreciation is part of your inheritance, if you like, you blockhead," said Frank, "and we will call again to-morrow, and take them to the theatre in the evening."

"Thanks, no," replied Cecil. "I must judge for myself in this matter, Frank, and I remember that I have a mother who is worthy of all honour, and who is known to this proud and prejudiced young lady. Our purpose however is answered by this call. I can now say that I have renewed my intimacy with the Mashams, and have been kindly received by both; my mother will be free from further persecution on that score. Come, let us find a dinner somewhere, and forget my 'parentage,' remembering only my 'education,' and the happy time it was to both of us."

"Well, let us try here," said Frank, as they reached the British Coffee-House, "and you shall let me see how far your mind has been improved by Uncle Sam."

The next morning brought Mr. Wycherly to London, and after a brief conversation with his daughter he announced to Mrs. Masham that Old Court was getting into a state of frightful disorder, owing to the absence of the presiding influence, and that Kate must pack up by the morrow to return home with him.

As Mr. Wycherly was known to have his own way when he desired it, this mandate was obeyed, and Ruth and her mother bade adieu to Kate, who certainly looked very unlike herself, and evidently required the air of her country home to restore freshness to her cheek and brightness to her eye. As Wycherly and Kate were driven away, Ruth held up her purple diary and nodded very knowingly. Kate frowned and shook her head. Frank was in despair for nearly half-an-hour when he heard of the sudden departure of the Wycherlys; but Ruth was dressed so becomingly and looked so very pretty at the time of his call, that he consoled himself by a rather vigorous flirtation, meeting with a very gentle reproof from Mrs. Masham. There was now no obstacle to Cecil's again visiting his aunt, but not all Ruth's simple cleverness could lead him to speak of Miss Wycherly, or to show an interest in anything which concerned her.

Frank, from force of habit, perhaps, was a more constant caller upon the Mashams than Cecil, and was always a welcome visitor, frequently escorting them to concerts, and showing such other attentions as were agreeable to the ladies. After a time, Cecil (how grave he had become!)

began to consider the possible consequences of this persistent attention on the part of his friend. Cecil saw danger to Ruth—to gentle, pretty Ruth, and he resolved to stand between her and sorrow, if it were not too late.

One night when he and Frank left the house after a pleasant chatty evening, he said :—

"Do you remember our drive to Holly Lodge the first time I went there?"

"Remember it—yes—let me see? We drove in our dog-cart, changing horses at Beechtree Hill. To be sure," replied Frank. "What of that?"

"Is that all you remember of it?" asked Cecil.

"Yes—about all. Why?"

"Can you recall a conversation we had on the danger of innocent flirtation with pretty girls?" said Cecil.

"Oh, to be sure—yes—quite well! You accused me of being a lady-killer, and of doing the agreeable to all the girls worth talking to," replied Frank laughing.

"And do you remember what you then said? That you were not a marrying man—that all women appeared to be alike to you?"

"Y-e-s," answered Frank, drawling out the word as though the question had set him thinking.

"Do you remember how you characterised the thoughtless trifler and the deliberate *roué?*" said Cecil, standing still and looking Frank in the face, upon which the light of a lamp shone strongly.

"Quite well; I spoke what I then felt, and what I still feel," replied Frank. "Why do you ask these questions?"

"Because, my good old Frank, I fear much that you have, without intending to do wrong, trifled with cousin Ruth, and have won more than you played for," said Cecil solemnly.

"Good heavens!" cried Frank, starting at the suggestion. "Surely you do not think that I have been so much misunderstood?"

"I do, almost to conviction, or I would not have

said it. Frank, I am young, very young, to have learned so much as I fancy I have done of the secrets of the heart, but thus it is, and my knowledge tells me that you have assumed so well the language, look, and bearing of a lover, that Ruth has believed your acting to be reality, and she has given you what she will never seek or be able to take back again—her first love."

Frank covered his face with his hands and leaned against the railings of a house. It was night, and as there were no passers-by in the street, Cecil let him remain undisturbed. At last he recovered himself sufficiently to speak.

"If what you say be true—if I have been so criminal—there is no other word—what will be thought of me? What shall I think of myself my whole life long?"

"You remember the name you once attached on such an offender, the night we rode down to Holly Lodge?" said Cecil calmly.

"I do! I do! never dreaming then that I should be called upon to say 'I am that villain!' I am terrified, Cecil, at my own unthinking cruelty. But perhaps it may not be as you surmise."

"It may not; but life is against that hope," said Cecil, speaking like a fate.

"It is! It is! And if it be true,—if I have gained that girl's love by pretending what seemed to be love for her, and then, believing that, were I to tell her she had deceived herself, I *should* do all that is wicked, base, and cruel. Cecil! friend! true friend, what course is open to me?"

"One—only one that you should follow, and if I know you, Frank, you will take no other," said Cecil, like an oracle of destiny.

Little more was said by either, and the friends parted for the night.

CHAPTER III.

FRANK UNDERGOES A SELF-EXAMINATION, AND THEN MEETS AN UNEXPECTED WITNESS TO CHARACTER.—FRIENDS IN COUNCIL.

THERE was a sterner questioner, a better-informed witness than Cecil Hartley, awaiting Frank in the solitude of his bed-chamber, and which he heard nearly the whole night long questioning and accusing. His own conscience recounted the incidents of every hour, almost, which he had passed with Ruth Masham; the flattering words which he had spoken without any other intention than to gratify his own weak desire of exciting her admiration and applause of himself, he not caring whether they died in her ear or lived in her heart; the many acts of marked courtesy which he had shown to win a smile into her pretty gentle face that he might have more pleasure from her beauty, heedless of their effect upon her to whom they would become memories which were to remain with her all her life long, and make up in a great degree the joy or sorrow of her existence. If Cecil's surmises were true she had so received them, and he had gained his pleasant victories at the expense of Ruth's love and peace. The accuser held to this against all the sophistry with which he sought to silence it. In vain he pleaded the absence of any evil thought or serious desire to make her regard him as other than an honest friend! He should have remembered that words have their natural meanings, and that one so unlearned in worldly knowledge as Ruth would understand them only in their simple significance, believing that he had spoken them as the utterance of truth, and if so, how must they have been understood by her?

Had he not said the like a hundred times before?

But never to such an auditor.

What had been his courtesies? A few small gifts—a few infrequent visits—until of late, and then Miss Wycherly had been present to account in part for his daily calls. He could not discontinue them when she had left without some assigned cause, and he had none. Why hold him accountable for wrong?

The accuser would not admit the pleas. Miss Wycherly repelled him whenever he had sought to flutter too near her, and always appeared to regard him only as the friend of Ruth, and not until Kate returned from her little tour and when she must have heard all which had passed during her absence, had she been perfectly unreserved with him, believing doubtlessly that the altered fortunes of her friend had removed all obstacles which might have interposed between them. He could but remember when he had observed the change in Miss Wycherly's behaviour to him. He perhaps had assigned a different cause for the change. If Kate had seen with Ruth's eyes and heard with Ruth's ears she could give evidence against him; and if he were guilty what course was open to him? Cecil had said there was only one; what was it?

Never to see Ruth again? To dispel the dream at once—rudely, decisively, and to tell her by that act how she had deceived herself—or, rather, how he had deceived her by his soft, winning words, and his pretty, heartless courtesies, and so an end? Could he believe that? Could he believe that the terrible conviction at which Ruth was to come would not be followed by such a weight of sorrow that it would crush all hope, all happiness out of her young heart, until in her gentle face and gentler eyes the presence would be seen of a slowly approaching death, or, what were a sadder fate, the evidences of unchangeable mourning for her blighted love? He had heard and read such stories often, and regarded them as painful fictions; but he remembered that, when he and his mother sat alone on the evening of the day when he had laid his father in the narrow house, that mother had told him how dear, how very dear, the dead had been to her, and that once on a time, before she was his wife, she had, from mere waywardness, vexed him greatly; and, though he loved her fondly then, he could but resent the pain she had given him without a cause, and kept away from her, as though he had closed his heart against one so unworthy of his love! What grief she suffered then! What terrible fear that he would not return again—that he, her first love, who had the whole happiness of her life in his keeping, would come to her no more! The agony of those days which intervened between the wrong and its forgiveness! The inexpressible thankfulness with which his restored tenderness was welcomed by the wayward girl who had so trifled with her peace was remembered still, even now when he could return no more, although her remaining life would be full of happy memories due to his unchanging love. Yes, he would return no more; she never should look into his face again, nor hear his voice again, nor his footstep on the stair; and his place at his hearth would be vacant for ever, let who might sit in his chair. When she had thought that such a time might come, she had wept and prayed to die before such desolation came. But now that it had arrived she desired to live, though much of the happiness which she had known through him was buried in his grave, and though the acuteness of her grief might last until she was laid beside him. Yes, she desired to live, for God had blessed her with another love, which was as pure and holy as that which Death had sanctified—her mother's love for him, her darling son, the still enduring joy, united with the past and present. As his father was true and just, so would be her son, never pausing to do right whatever might be the cost or the sacrifice of self.

Again conscience questioned him. If Cecil's surmises are correct, what course should be yours?

One answer only came. To marry without love, to drag through life the heaviest chain which man or woman wears, although its links may be of gold—to play the hypocrite from day to day, when taken at the best, traitor or brute when care for self predominates,—or to cast away the gentle, trusting Ruth to the certain misery of a betrayed love. Fearful alternatives!

Worn out at length by the terrible conflict of his thoughts, Frank fell into a sleep which was not rest, for the excited brain kept labouring with fantastic dreams through the few remaining hours of the night.

Fortunately for Frank, his mother did not join him at breakfast, as she would have seen how wan and woebegone he looked, and would as surely have enquired the cause. He therefore bade her good morning at the door of her bedchamber, and went on his way to the City, not taking his usual route, and thereby avoiding the chance of seeing Ruth at the window, where she usually sat to give him a "morning greeting."

Poor Ruth! there was a little cloud on her gentle face when the well-timed omnibus passed without the admired occupant of the knifeboard.

As Frank walked briskly on, the fresh air of the morning and the quickened circulation of his blood dispelled much of the despondency which had oppressed him, and he began to question the correctness of Cecil's surmises, for they were only surmises, and to attribute them more to Cecil's sensitive temperament than to incontrovertible deductions from facts. Ruth had never shown that she entertained a strong feeling for him, or accorded any other reception to his attentions than was consonant with the close intimacy which had grown up between them, and he might have been disquieting himself in vain. He could put her to the test by absenting himself from her society, and if she appeared to be indifferent, he would be most careful in his bearing to her for the future. If he had indeed won her love, what was he bound to do? The happiness of one or the other must be sacrificed, for though he admired her beauty, and respected her gentleness of character, he knew that he did not love her as he would have desired to love the woman he could call his wife, in sincerity and truth. If Ruth loved him as his mother had loved his dead father, and he should abandon her, she was destined to lose all the joy and hopes of her young life, and to bear into whatever future there was ordained for her, nothing but regrets, until what should have been the sweetness of her existence would turn to poison, killing slowly but surely. If one then must suffer, it should be he, the unwitting offender. Honour, self-respect, all that makes life of value truly, demanded that such should be his course, and he would have to conceal the absence of love by the aid of an ever-watchful tenderness, which would continue to deceive her into the belief that they had exchanged hearts as well as vows when they had united hands. The task would not be difficult, he thought, and whatever he might lose by marrying Ruth without experiencing that indefinable desire which should unite two wedded lives, would be in part made up to him by the conviction that he was repaying her in the love she had given him, and by the comfort of an approving conscience. But he would be satisfied.

The required evidence would soon be abundantly supplied, silently at first, and then by revelations which could not be misunderstood.

Three mornings had passed, and Hero had watched for Leander, who came not, neither had he called for the evening's pleasant chat, and Mrs. Masham at last expressed her surprise at Mr. Lockyer's singular absence. She asked Cecil if his friend had left London; and there was something so hesitating and constrained in the manner and phrases of Cecil, that Ruth did not fail to be struck by them, although her mother was satisfied by the explanatory conjectures which were hazarded to account for Frank's defection, as it were, from their circle. The consciousness of what he had observed, and of the conversation which he had had with Frank, made Cecil equally observant of the effect of his words upon Ruth; and as he became more than ever satisfied that his conjectures as to the state of his poor cousin were correct, he resolved to bring matters to an issue with Frank even at the cost of disturbance of their long friendship. With this intention he called at Frank's place of business on the following day, and was surprised and pained to find that he had gone into the country very unexpectedly, on some unexplained business, affecting, he had said, the interests of his family. Such unusual conduct towards Cecil could bear only one construction, and that was very unfavourable to the absentee.

So marked a change came over Ruth that her mother was greatly disturbed, and attributed it to her London dissipation, as she called it, and resolved to return at once to Old Court, where the Wycherlys were prepared to receive them. Poor Ruth urged nothing against this proposition of her mother. What could she say? She could hardly account to herself for the restlessness which oppressed her, or why on a sudden all which had interested her in the busy streets had ceased to attract her notice almost, and allowed her to sit gazing listlessly from her window, having eyes only for the past.

The "family business" of Mr. Frank Lockyer was only "fudge." He had referred to the time-table of one of the new railways, packed up a portmanteau and his fishing-gear, and departed by an early train for a station whose name appeared familiar to him, some forty miles from London. Having taken up his quarters at a little inn in a village near to the station, he obtained, by the good offices of his landlord, permission to fish in a neighbouring stream, and thither he went daily, more to hold undisturbed communion with himself than to exercise the gentle craft, returning to a late dinner, and usually with a very ill-filled basket. The results of these self-examinations were perplexingly conflicting. Sometimes he succeeded in convincing himself that Cecil had been deceived, and that Ruth's heart was untouched. At others, he believed that his conduct had been undoubtedly inconsiderate, and that an atonement was due from him; but whatever the conclusion at which he had arrived, Kate Wycherly had been always in his presence, and had either increased the pain of the self-sacrifice which he contemplated, or stimulated him to avoid dishonour by acting justly to her friend. It had been so from the first, even from the night when Cecil had awakened him to a sense of his own peril and Ruth's wrong. Would that subtle influence pass away, or remain with him for years to come?

One afternoon or evening rather, for the church clock had struck six, Frank was sauntering homeward, when he came suddenly upon a brother angler patiently bobbing for eels, and who had been rewarded with but little better success than himself. Anglers are generally attracted to each other, and Frank and the bobber soon became conversational, the more so as both were tired of their sport, and the homeward way was to the same village. Frank was interested in his companion, as he talked like a man of some education, and there was something of the poor gentleman about him, despite his homely faded suit of pepper-and-salt, and not over clean linen. When they arrived at the little inn where Frank's dinner was waiting him, he pressed his new acquaintance to join him as a guest, but the stranger declined the invitation, as he had already dined, promising however to return in the evening for an hour's chat over a pipe of tobacco. As the stranger removed his hat at parting, Frank saw that the right side of his flaxen hair was streaked with black lines, and he would have known by those indications, had he been as well informed as you, dear reader, that his new acquaintance was no other than Mr. Jeffery Garrett, the village schoolmaster. Frank might have learned this readily enough had he been curious in the matter, by questioning his host, but his dinner was waiting, and youth, even in tribulation, rarely loses its appetite.

Mr. Garrett was punctual to his appointment, and the two anglers chatted over many subjects beside the sport which had brought them together, until they arrived at those personal confidences which frequently attend long sittings over tobacco and any generous liquid accompaniment.

"Yes, sir," said Jeffery, "I am a bachelor, and likely to continue so. Not my own fault either, as time was when I was willing to marry, and fancied I had found one who liked me well enough for a husband. But it was not to be, sir. It was not to be."

"Sorrow is dry," says the adage, and Jeffery gave convincing proof of its truth by a copious imbibition.

"The lady died, I presume?" asked Frank.

"No, sir; she had a fine constitution, and is still living. She transferred her affections to my cousin, and I broke down under my disappointment. I was never a man afterwards."

"The jilt!" said Frank, rather seriously, wondering, at the same time, how such a queer, rusty-looking fellow as Jerry was then, could have ever loved so well.

"Yes, sir. I'm afraid we must call her a flirt—a prettier word than jilt, sir, with nearly the same signification—I thought—do think still, that she loved me once, judging by the ordinary indications in such matters. But I might have been deceived, for she dismissed me with less ceremony than she would have parted with a scullion; not even a week's notice, sir. I was requested to keep out of the bar-parlour on the very day I had resolved to make her a formal proposal, and in less than a week my cousin—my cousin stayed to tea and supper, and ultimately published banns and married her."

"Surely such a girl was not worth the regret of a moment," said Frank cheerily, seeing that Jeffery was allowing the ashes of his pipe to mingle with the pepper and salt of his trousers.

"You mustn't say that, if you please, sir, even

at this distance of time," remarked Jerry. "She was worthy all the love I gave her, and made an excellent wife and an exemplary mother. I forgave her long ago, for I fancy vacillation ran in the family. Her mother broke with an old love to marry Mereweather. Women think nothing of that! Love sits easy with them."

"Mereweather!" said Frank.

"Yes. Hester's mother's name was Mereweather. Hester married a cousin of mine who died, poor fellow! and left her a widow with an only child. She had a hard fight for some years, and gallantly she did it. Fortune has smiled on her at last, and I am very glad that Hester has been cared for at last."

Frank knew his new friend now, although he did not tell him so. He knew not why he kept silence as to his knowledge of Jeffery's kindred, but he felt like a guilty man who feared to speak, lest the words he should utter might be remembered to his disadvantage. He was fortunately relieved from further conversation by the clock striking ten and warning Jeffery that it was time to say "Good night."

When he had gone, Frank went to his bed also, again to summon to his pillow the witness and the accuser, but this time Ruth was to be arraigned, and the value of her love tried at the visionary tribunal.

Was she not Hester's daughter who had loved so lightly, and married so readily, not the first choice of her maiden heart, but the richer, bolder wooer?

Was she as vacillating as her forebears had proved to be, and might she not have been as lightly won, to suffer no scathe, no sorrow beyond a few transient tears, which some new lover would dry speedily?

Accuser and witness had both spoken that night by the mouth of one of her own kin. Spoken so strangely as though to warn him not to commit his future too rashly, urged on by the prompting of what might be after all conjecture only. He was glad that he had not been more communicative to Jeffery, and with that thought he fell asleep.

Hitherto he had hesitated to write to Cecil, fearing to confess, even to his dearest friend, all that his conscience urged against himself, and the course of conduct which it indicated as the only one he could pursue in honour and justice. Now, he had, he thought, discovered a claim to have his own happiness considered before he accepted the hard conditions which his thoughtlessness appeared to impose. He therefore wrote to Cecil at great length all that he could recall of his self-communings, as we have already recorded them, reserving nothing either for or against himself, and concluding by earnestly entreating his friend's honest consideration of them, and his plain, truthful counsel.

Cecil received this long communication with both pleasure and pain. With pleasure that Frank had lost none of his old confidence in him; with pain that what Frank regarded as a great self-sacrifice would probably be required of him. Cecil considered carefully every line of Frank's letter, and then replied to it.

"You have reflected"—he wrote,—"upon this matter, as I believed you would. You have acted as I hope I should have done had I been placed in the same painful position. You are right to require the fullest satisfaction that you have committed the great wrong which demands so great an atonement; and though you can only arrive at conviction by the infliction of serious pain to Ruth, the sacrifice you are prepared to make when satisfied that it is deserved, justifies the experiment. The knowledge that you have demanded and received those proofs of her devoted love (should it exist) will increase her claims upon your sympathy and after tenderness, and make your own state more happy. You may yet bring yourself to accept her love, her gentleness, at their great value, and believe that you might have chosen another where those enduring virtues had been wanting. You might, dear friend, have elected to be free, and silenced your conscience by the absence of intention to transgress, by your own honest convictions that you had never sought the love of Ruth, and that her sorrows were of her own creating. Few in the world would have blamed such a selfish determination. But could you know (as you would know), and be at peace, that your careless words, your loving acts, had cheated her into a belief that her love had been asked of her by you, and when the deceit was discovered, nothing was left to her for all her remaining days—be they few or many—but such indescribable regrets as would destroy every blessing of her life and make death a welcome liberator. I for one believe that hearts will break—not by a sharp cruel spasm which ends all sufferings, but by a lasting, sickening grief which keeps possession of the mind sleeping or waking, mingling with every pleasant hour that comes between our promised sorrows, making them more bitter and hopeless than they would be; for all have their portion of recurrent good, if man would not destroy his own inheritance. And such enduring grief is slaying many gentle hearts, whose pure, true, early love has been rejected or betrayed.

"If Ruth loves you, you could not endure, I know, that such a grief should have been planted in her heart by your hand—no! although it had been done in sport.

"I say no word for Ruth. Let her love be tried, and for the sake of both I trust my conviction may prove to be a delusion. But I fancy the trial has begun.

"I have read what I have written. It is somewhat like playhouse rant, but every word has had an echo in my own heart. Yes, my true, my only friend (except my dear mother), I love—love hopelessly, and know I have a sorrow which will be my companion to the end. Can you not guess whom I love? Must I write her name to you—the proud, prejudiced girl who would kill me (if she could) with a look did I tell her that I loved her? 'Man's love,' says Byron, 'is of man's soul a thing apart.' I tell you what. That man wrote too much about love ever to have known it. Not that I intend to break my heart if I can help it."

Possibly we also may have written enough about love, for the present.

CHAPTER IV.

MRS. MASHAM LEARNS RUTH'S SECRET, AND SHE AND KATE TAKE COUNSEL TOGETHER.—MR. WYCHERLY RECEIVES INSTRUCTIONS.

THE return of Ruth to her native air did not bring back freshness to her cheek nor lightness to her step. Her mother marked the change, without suspecting the cause, and Ruth always answered her enquiries with a gentle smile—it had more sadness in it every day—and called her mother's fears only loving fancies. Ruth rarely remained alone with her mother, as though she feared her questioning, and from Kate she was as rarely apart, knowing that there was no secrecy between them, and that her dear, true friend was the only one at Old Court of whose sympathy she was certain. She could not have confessed to her mother, who had watched her daily life with such tenderness, who had lived only for her, that she had become sated with the old affection, and desired to exchange it for another love. She could not confess to her that she had given away her maiden heart to one who had only asked it by gentle acts and vague words, which she had perhaps interpreted wrongly. O if she had! If she had believed, without cause, that he loved her! O if she had done that! And as this terrible thought arose in her mind more frequently day by day, her face grew sadder and her eyes gazed vacantly as though she saw only the pleasant past or the desolate future. These painful abstractions became so recurrent at length that Kate found it difficult to find consolatory words to rouse her into any hopefulness, and at last she said to Ruth:

"I am going to be very angry with you—very;" but her face was so full of tenderness as she said this, that Ruth smiled, and looked enquiringly at her.

"Indeed, indeed, my dear girl, you are acting most unjustly to yourself—most unjustly, I hope, to Mr. Lockyer—by the despondency which you encourage, despite my efforts to dispel it. I tell you again there is nothing surprising in this sudden absence. Business men are often called away at a moment's notice. I have learned this from my father, and you should remember that though Mr. Lockyer has shown you such unmistakeable attention, and spoken so very plainly, he has not yet obtained either your permission or your mother's to be considered as your accepted lover."

"And that is why I fear so much that I have been mistaken in what has passed between us," said Ruth, her full eyes filled with tears. "I may have deceived myself, and given him my love before he has asked it."

"No, Ruth—if words have meaning—if acts have meaning also—Mr. Lockyer has declared unmistakeably that he loves you, or at least he has made you—made me believe so. He cannot be so wicked as to have trifled with your peace and his own honour so long and constantly."

"I cannot think him so wicked—I will not think him so cruel, so dishonourable," cried Ruth, clasping her hands together. "I will trust to Him who knows how purely, how disinterestedly I love him, that I shall be spared such bitter sorrow as would come to me, if we are deceived in Frank Lockyer!" and then she threw her arms around Kate's neck, and gave way to a passion of tears.

"You are right so to believe, dear Ruth," replied Kate, pressing the recumbent head to her own heaving bosom. "If you had, from girlish vanity, sought to win from him his pleasant attention and grateful services, you might doubt that they were offered only as ordinary civilities, but being unsought by you, it is right that you receive this man's words and acts as truth, and accept them as you have done—not lightly."

Ruth looked up into her true friend's face,

smiling through her tears, and then kissed Kate tenderly.

The interview we have described took place in a large summer-house in a secluded part of the garden, and one of the windows was open, looking upon a path but little used excepting by the work-people. Through this window Kate saw that Mrs. Masham had been an observer, if not a hearer of what had taken place. Yes: it was evident that Ruth's secret was betrayed to her mother, for Mrs. Masham was weeping, and she motioned Kate to be silent as to her presence, before she walked stealthily away. Kate was glad that this discovery had been made, as, knowing how dearly Ruth's mother loved her child, there would be more sympathy and better guidance perhaps for her love-stricken friend, than her own inexperience could offer. As soon as Ruth was sufficiently composed the two friends returned to the house. As they approached it Kate saw that Mrs. Masham was watching for them, although apparently busied in attending to the flowers in one of the bay windows. The two girls did not enter the room where she was, but went at once to that which they occupied together, and did not come down to the drawing-room until Kate had declared Ruth's face to be free from all traces of her recent excitement. Mrs. Masham held a book in her hand, but thoughts in which the volume had no share had evidently engrossed her, for when the two friends entered the room, she started slightly at their approach. Immediately recovering her self-possession, she said carelessly: "Well, my dears, tired of each other's society at last. I was afraid I was to be forgotten for the rest of the evening."

Ruth ran to her and kissed her, patting her cheeks and calling her "a naughty mamma for thinking so." Some other "pretty prattle" succeeded, until Ruth seated herself at the piano, and played one of the airs which *somebody* had given her—how long ago it seemed! Whilst Ruth was thus engaged, Mrs. Masham having written upon a piece of paper handed it to Kate.

There was more sorrow in her still handsome face than Kate had ever seen there before.

The paper contained only two lines:—

"DEAR KATE,—You must, please, see me alone, either before or after we go to bed. You will?"

Kate having read what was written, added the word "after," and returned the paper—poor Ruth little thinking, whilst her nimble fingers flew over the responsive keys, and her heart vibrated with every note, what a dreadful conspiracy was in progress behind her back.

There was a strange constraint felt by all, until the return of Mr. Wycherly from Hilltown, where he had been detained on business which had apparently required the discussion of a certain modicum of wine as well as the dry commercial details of the transaction, and he so completely monopolised the conversation for the rest of the evening, that there was no occasion for either of the ladies to break the silence which was now so agreeable to them, until they bade each other

“Good-night,” leaving Mr. Wycherly to finish his cigar over which he had already nodded a dozen times, to the great danger of his shirt frill, then protruding more than was consistent with its ordinary respectability.

It was a lovely moonlight night, and the two friends usually sat at the open window of their dressing-room, looking out upon the distant lights of Hilltown and the intervening valley. To-night however Kate urged Ruth to go at once to her bed, reminding her of the excitement she had undergone, and the necessity she had for repose. Ruth obeyed reluctantly, but Kate as she sat beside her bed had soon the satisfaction of seeing that sleep had “sealed up” her eyes, and that she was in the land of dreams—of happy dreams she hoped. Kate then went as noiselessly as possible to Mrs. Masham's room, and found her anxiously expecting her.

“Thanks, dear Kate, for coming to me so soon. I was afraid you would have been at least an hour later, and every minute seemed ten times told since I have been expecting you. You know of course why I have asked to see you. You will believe that what I saw and overheard was the result of chance—not of design. I would not willingly have learned Ruth's secret by such meanness. You believe this?"

"I do, indeed," replied Kate, taking the hand which Mrs. Masham offered to her.

"I am glad to have known what I do—very glad, though it has given me more pain than I have ever known of my Ruth's making. If I heard rightly, Ruth has formed an attachment for Frank Lockyer. Am I right?"

"I betray nothing in saying 'Yes,'" replied Kate.

"When did he propose to her?" asked Mrs. Masham, somewhat sternly.

"O, long ago: at least—I believe—some months ago," replied Kate, hesitatingly.

"And why did I not know it? Why was I, her mother, not informed of such a proceeding, which concerns Ruth's happiness so greatly? Why was her confidence withheld from me?" Mrs. Masham asked with quick utterances.

Kate knew not what to say. Frank had never made any formal declaration of his love: it had shown itself in his acts and words generally, and this Kate was compelled at last to admit to Mrs. Masham.

"There is a painful satisfaction in hearing what you say," she replied, her tears falling fast. "I am relieved to know that Ruth has not withheld from me such an important confidence. The rest is bad enough to learn, but I think I never could have forgiven—I mean never have forgotten—such mistrust in the child I love so dearly."

"You know I have spoken truly," said Kate, putting her arm round the neck of the weeping mother. "I could not have been a party to any concealment of such a matter from you, nor could dear Ruth either, but as this feeling grew up insensibly—imperceptibly—there seemed nothing to confide—nothing but what you could have observed—which was unsuspected by Ruth until it betrayed itself to her when Mr. Lockyer so suddenly—so strangely, I will say—absented himself from your house."

"I ought to have been more watchful—more careful," said Mrs. Masham. "I alone am to blame. I ought to have remembered how sensitive, how susceptible of any kindness Ruth was, and foreseen that what were, I believe and fear, only common civilities on the part of Lockyer, might be mistaken as they have been. I might have saved my darling child the pain of loving where she may be unloved."

"She is loved," cried Kate, earnestly. "I am sure of that, if Frank Lockyer is not utterly deceitful and designing. Cecil Hartley has said again and again that he was the soul of honour."

"Cecil speaks of his friend as man speaks of man in their relation to each other, not as between man and woman," replied Mrs. Masham. "What would they both have a right to say? Mr. Lockyer has been very kind, very civil, but he has never thought of making love as it is called. What claim has Ruth upon him?"

"Claim?" asked Kate, reddening. "She can claim to have understood his words as they were spoken, and his acts as they were meant. If he denies that he intended to win her regard—her love, I will say—then he is a contemptible trifler; and if I were Ruth I would cast him away without a regret."

"But Ruth has not your strength of will, your power of self-control," replied Mrs. Masham. "A fire such as has been lighted in Ruth's heart, you could crush out at will. It will destroy Ruth."

"It will bless her whole life if I augur rightly," said Kate. "But the truth must be known at once," she added, after a pause.

"Known at once! How?" asked Mrs. Masham, surprised at Kate's emphatic manner.

"Mr. Lockyer must be required to speak out," said Kate, compressing her lips and shaking her head as though she had the delinquent before her, and was addressing him.

"Good heavens! You would not have Ruth make the first advance?" asked Mrs. Masham. "You would not have her confess to having a love for this man, who would then be justified indeed in rejecting her."

No; Kate would not ask that. Her own maiden instincts revolted at such a supposition, and she felt that it would be better to die the daily death of the unhappy than expose her gentle friend to such an ordeal.

The conversation ceased for a while, and both the speakers appeared content with their own thoughts, the mother seeing only the dark future of her child, the friend seeking some bright opening in the present.

"Light at last," cried Kate, in a suppressed voice, and clapping her hands noiselessly together. "My father must be appealed to: he must be Ruth's father also in this matter. He has invited Mr. Lockyer to shoot at Old Court, and out of that circumstance—I don't clearly see how, at present—we shall arrive at the truth. Not a word more, dear Mrs. Masham—not another word to-night. We will take counsel together again in the morning. I will ask my father to invite Ruth to a drive, and we can then talk quietly over the matter. Good-night."

Kate reached her room without disturbing any one, and as her light fell upon the head of Ruth, she saw that her face was as peaceful as though the angels had been with her since she had fallen asleep.

In the morning the plan of the preceding night was put into operation. Ruth went for her drive, and the conference was held, whereat it was agreed that, as Mr. Lockyer was to be a guest at Old Court for a day or two, and during the visit of the Mashams, Mr. Wycherly should be instructed to act as the next friend of the family, and put certain enquiries to the young gentleman, in manner to be hereafter specified.

In accordance with this resolution, Kate requested a private audience of her father in his own room, and thereat she made him fully acquainted with much that the reader already knows concerning Ruth and Frank Lockyer.

"And now," continued Kate, "we think it is in your power to end these painful doubts, by requiring from Mr. Lockyer an explanation of the marked attentions which he has paid to Ruth."

"Ask me to turn match-maker!" exclaimed Wycherly. "What right have I to interfere?"

"No right, certainly of your own accord," said Kate, calmly; "but it is a duty you owe to Mrs. Masham, and I know you will undertake it."

"How a duty?" asked Wycherly, getting very red, and speaking loudly.

Kate was used to her father's impetuosity of temper, and therefore was not disturbed by it now.

"I believe that it was at your earnest persuasion that Mrs. Masham became the proprietor of the 'Rosebush.' She for some time objected to your proposal; for seeing that by acceding to it she risked the possibility of exposing Ruth to other intimacies than those she would have selected for her——"

"Why, what the deuce——"

"Hear me to the end," continued Kate. "What she feared has come to pass. Through her connection with the Rosebush, this intimacy with Mr. Lockyer has arisen, and become the cause of great anxiety to Ruth and to her mother."

"But what had I——"

"Again I must ask you to be patient," said Kate, calmly. "By your kind indulgence, Ruth has become my dearest friend, and I know that the happiness of her life is at stake at this time, and that you are the only person besides Mr. Lockyer who can help to make her happy."

"How, Kate? How? I can't take the fellow by the collar, drag him to church, and make him marry her," said Wycherly.

"Nor are you asked to do anything so

ridiculous and impossible, my dear father. All I ask of you is to perform an act of friendliness to those unfriended women. You have invited Mr. Lockyer down for a day or two's shooting, have you not?"

"Yes, I have, and I ought to write to remind him of the invitation," said Wycherly, glad to turn the conversation.

"You must not write to him," continued Kate. "You must see him, and say that as Miss Masham is staying with me, you think it only your duty to request an explanation as to his presumed relations with——"

"What, tell him that Ruth is in love with him?"

"No, father. Ruth would rather die than have such a revelation made to Mr. Lockyer. He would despise her very properly, were such an admission to be made. Ruth has not any knowledge of what I am now doing, or her gentle nature would be too much shocked ever to forgive even me, perhaps—of that I am certain." Kate sighed deeply, and rested her head upon her hand for a few moments.

"I really can't see what good I can do," said her father. "If the man is in love he will say so, I presume; and if he is not, why, Ruth must pluck up a spirit and forget him."

"Do you think that would be possible?" asked Kate tenderly. "Do you not know that it would be impossible, supposing she really loves?"

Before Wycherly replied he looked up at the portrait of his lost wife which hung before him, and in a voice tremulous and subdued, said, "Yes —impossible."

Kate knew the direction his thoughts had taken, and she rose up, went to him, and placed her arms about his neck, and so continued to embrace him until their conversation was nearly ended.

"If you can save poor Ruth from such regrets as will overtake her should she continue to encourage what may prove a hopeless love, will you not do it? Mr. Lockyer has suddenly withdrawn from visiting her, and it is well that we know the reason."

"We will know the reason, Kate. I will call upon him and ask him plainly why he has acted so strangely. He must know, as you have said, that Ruth loves him——"

"Not a word of that to him, father," said Kate earnestly.

"Why not speak the truth?" replied her father. "Why should this poor girl fret herself into a consumption perhaps from her love to this fellow, when a few plain words might save her?"

"They would not save her, even if they produced the good you imagine they might do. Women are proud of their love, and would not see it humbled even before those to whom they would give it freely if it were asked of them."

"Then what am I to do?" asked Wycherly, at his wits' end.

"Your course is a very plain one," replied Kate. "You have only to see Mr. Lockyer, and speak to him as from yourself. You have to tell him that

Miss Masham will be here during his visit to Old Court, and that having heard and seen how constantly he has visited her—how kind he has been in a hundred ways—you are fearful that, as she is of a gentle, loving nature, there is danger of her misinterpreting such marked attentions, and that as you her only friend almost would not willingly expose her to such danger, you have thought it your duty to be thus explicit, and to request him to forego his visit, if you have misunderstood the relations he desires to establish with the Mashams."

Kate said this so deliberately, so calmly, that Wycherly sat dumbfounded for some moments. He could not believe for some time that his daughter Kate, who had scarcely peeped into the great world outside Old Court, could have been so diplomatic, so learned in the art of worming out the hidden secrets of politic man, and bringing him to honest confession. Kate did not wait for a reply, but taking advantage of her father's confusion, went on.

"You now see how easy is the task required of you. Mr. Lockyer is away from London at present, I believe; but you will be going to town in a week or two, and you can inquire about him at his office."

"And suppose he should tell me that he has only been amusing himself at Ruth's expense," asked Wycherly when he could speak.

"You have then only to bid him good-day," said Ruth, adding solemnly, "and leave the rest to Him who tempers the wind to the shorn lamb."

"No, I shall not. I shall tell him he's a heartless scoundrel that I should like to tie to a cart's-tail and belabour until I was tired," replied Wycherly. "I have not much faith in him."

"I have," said Kate again calmly. "Those who have known him long, speak of him as a true friend and a good son; and a man who deserves those titles is not likely to trifle with a woman's love."

"I suppose you have heard that character of

him from that Cecil Hartley," said Wycherly. "'Birds of a feather' is not a bad adage."

"I believe not," said Kate scarcely above a whisper.

"And if ever there was a rogue who deserved hanging, and escaped the gallows, that Jacob Selwyn Hartley is the one."

"We have nothing to do with him at present," said Kate, unclasping her arms. "Mrs. Masham is sure to hear when Mr. Lockyer returns, should you not find him when you call in London."

"Well, I am mightily afraid," said Wycherly, "that I shall make a mess of this business. It is difficult enough to make love on your own account——"

"But you are not going to make love," interrupted Kate.

"Very much the same thing, my dear. Making another man declare himself is doing the thing by proxy. Well, I must do as you desire, I suppose," said Wycherly resignedly.

"You are a dear, good papa, and there are two

kisses in part of the hundred you shall have if you manage our business cleverly." And so ended the interview between Kate and her father.

Mrs. Masham did hear in a few days of Frank Lockyer's return from the country, but Mr. Wycherly was not informed that the intelligence came in a letter from Cecil to his Aunt Hester, in case the prejudiced old gentleman should have doubted its accuracy and delayed his visit to London, which was now hastened by the importunity of his daughter Kate.

CHAPTER V.

THE AMBASSADOR HAS AN AUDIENCE, AND GAINS NOTHING BY HIS DIPLOMACY—FRANK TAKES COUNSEL OF HIS MOTHER.

PERPLEXED, irresolute, and unhappy, Frank Lockyer returned to London, and heard with increased pain from Cecil of the departure of Ruth and her mother, although the information of their visit to Old Court was unaccompanied by any inferences as to the cause or the motives which had influenced Mrs. Masham in her determination to leave London. Cecil had done his *devoirs* for Ruth, and now waited the revelations of time.

An invitation from Mr. Wycherly, therefore, requesting Frank to dine with him at the Bedford Hotel in Covent Garden (a favourite resort of country gentlemen), did not fail to connect itself with Ruth, as Cecil's reserve had been rightly interpreted by his friend; and Mr. Wycherly's summons, though unexpected, was no doubt the prelude to some further information. The invitation was therefore accepted, and Frank's suspicions were confirmed by the evident embarrassment of Wycherly, which continued throughout the time of dinner, and until their after wine had been rather freely circulated.

"Mr. Lockyer," said Wycherly, after a pause and several hems, which Frank understood as heralding the real business of their meeting, "Mr. Lockyer, I have been looking to your visit to Old Court with much pleasure — until lately, very lately, I may say."

"May I ask what has produced the change?" asked Frank smiling.

"Yes—you may; and in fact it was to tell you that, and partly to remind you of your promise to visit us, that I asked you to meet me here."

Mr. Wycherly then repeated as nearly as he could remember the formula which Kate had arranged on the evening of their first consultation, and which she had repeated to him on every convenient occasion afterwards, until she concluded that her ambassador could make no serious mistake in the discharge of his mission.

"Your consideration for your friend," replied Frank, "is very natural—very proper; although I should be glad to know if you alone have construed my civilities into marked attentions deserving to be questioned."

"If you mean by that," said Wycherly, rather disappointed at not receiving a frank acknowledgment or a plain denial of the correctness of Kate's surmises, "if you mean by that, whether others have noticed your attentions to Ruth,—I say yes—certainly yes."

"Her cousin Cecil Hartley perhaps?" said Frank inquiringly.

"No, sir!" answered Wycherly sharply; "I have no intimacy with Mr. Hartley,—I mean I have not seen your friend for some time."

Frank had been unfortunate in his guess, as

Mr. Wycherly instantly proceeded in his own mind to connect all his personal dislikes to the Hartleys with the young man whose confidence he had expected to have obtained with less difficulty than seemed likely to be the case at present.

"Has Mrs. Masham judged of my conduct as you seem to do?" asked Frank, without looking up.

"I don't know what Mrs. Masham has done," replied Wycherly quickly; "though I suppose she has not been more blind than other people; but my daughter—Kate, sir—has thought with me that this interview was desirable."

"Miss Wycherly thinks so?" said Frank, more to himself than to her father; adding, "Does Miss Wycherly see with her own eyes, think you?"

"Of course she does! Whose eyes do you think she uses but her own?" answered Wycherly. "Now, Mr. Lockyer, let us be plain with each other. I am not in the habit of beating about the bushes, when by boldly walking into them I can fairly start my game, though a few scratches may be the consequences. I therefore ask you, have your attentions to Ruth Masham any serious meaning? or have you been only philandering like "——the speaker paused——"like—— "

Frank looked inquiringly in his face.

"Well, sir, like a heartless jackanapes, who, to while away an idle hour, has trifled with the peace of a gentle, loving girl, and only deserves a horsepond?"

"You speak somewhat too warmly, sir; but your age and position give you privileges," said Frank rising. "I will think over our conversation, and write to you to-morrow."

"Very well; though I should have imagined you had already thought, seriously thought, over the subject. Perhaps your answer had better be given in writing, as a personal reply might not be very pleasant to either of us."

"You must put your own construction on my hesitation, Mr. Wycherly; and I hope you will allow upon reflection that I have shown some patience during this interview. If you will allow me, I will ring the bell and wish you a good-night."

"As you please," replied Wycherly, jerking the bell-pull violently. "If I have said anything offensive—anything which I should not have said—I ask you to excuse it, unless —— "

"Unless," said Frank, bowing and smiling, "I prove a philandering jackanapes, and then, I presume, I am welcome to the horsepond. Good night, sir. We may yet laugh over this meeting.

Wycherly gave a curt "Good-night," and then resumed his cigar, which he had thrown down in the heat of conversation.

"I wish Kate had not driven me into this business! I knew I couldn't coax the fellow into an admission of his honesty or rascality. I knew I should speak out as I have done, and perhaps made mischief where I ought to have been ready to have smoothed away difficulties."

It was scarcely ten o'clock, and as he could

not sit smoking and drinking by himself he strolled out into the Piazza, and watched the wretched pariahs who haunt the Garden, flitting here and there, now asking alms, now turning summersaults, or dodging heavy-heeled policemen, until he wondered if the ghosts of the old monks of Westminster ever revisited their once-secluded grounds and joined the choristers at Evans's! The wine, or the discussion, or both combined had evidently obfuscated Mr. Wycherly, and accounted in part for the temper he had displayed, and of which Frank had been so tolerant.

Mr. Wycherly's walk terminating at the entrance to "Evans's,'" he descended the steps of that world-famed hostelry, and found himself in a low, long room filled with visitors, over whom presided a tall, round-faced man, who divided his attention between stimulating his guests to give their orders, and amusing some young prodigals who were advertising their incompetency by drinking champagne and making considerably more noise than was decorous.

We must not confound the "Evans's" of our story and its coarse songs and limited accommodation with the present popular establishment, conducted by the most urbane of hosts, who is not tall in stature, and whose good-humoured face, supported by the whitest of shirt-collars, blushes even redder than health has made it, at any mention of the improprieties of his predecessor.

The "Evans's" of to-day is a sort of chapel-of-ease to the London clubs, and there may be found at fitting times members of all the professions, who resort thither sure of the same immunity from annoyance as they would find in their own smoking-rooms. Not unfrequently, it is believed, very great ladies safely indulge their curiosity about men's amusements by visiting a certain private box, where, as carefully screened from observation as they would be behind the lattice of the hareem of a sultan, they even partake of the "specialities" of the house, whilst listening to well-sung madrigals and other noises of sweet music.

But it is with Mr. Wycherly and the "Evans's"

of the past we have now to do, and with a person —you could not call him a gentleman—who sat next to Wycherly, regarding him from time to time rather furtively. He was showily dressed, and appeared to be conscious of the whiteness and evenness of his teeth, as he made a full display of them whenever his lips were relieved of the cigar which he was smoking. Finding that his neighbour made no advances towards conversation, he took the initiative, by remarking at the conclusion of a song :—

"Very good that—very well sung—though rather near the wind."

"If you mean rather coarse I agree with you," replied Wycherly. "Who's the singer?"

"I don't know, I am sure," replied the other. "I am not a regular frequenter, and only looked in to-night to oblige a cus—a friend. You are also a stranger, I fancy?"

"Yes, I live in the country near Hilltown," replied Wycherly, with that communicativeness for which provincial gentlemen are rather celebrated.

"Hilltown!" said the stranger; "I think I have heard of that place. Yes to be sure. When I was quite a lad I was there, I remember. It stands on the top of a hill with a valley all round it."

The acuteness of this remark did not appear to call for any comment, so Wycherly said:—

"Who did you know? I have lived there many years."

"Hem! I forget at the moment," answered the other, adding after a pause, "I knew, when he was living, a Mr. Lockyer, who had a place near there, I fancy."

"Oh yes, at Holly Lodge," said Wycherly; "though I knew but little of him, as he was generally laid up with the gout. Do you know his son?"

"Yes—that is, I did," replied the other. "But I don't encourage his acquaintance. He's a bit of a puppy—rather conceited of his good looks, and fond of aping the aristocracy. I've no great opinion of his commercial capacity, nor of him as a lot."

As Frank at that moment was not in high favour with Wycherly, this deprecatory opinion was rather satisfactory than otherwise, and so Wycherly said :—

"I am glad to have met you, sir, as I have a little business with that young gentleman, and a knowledge of his character may be of service to me."

"What I know of him is quite at your service," replied the stranger. "Allow me to offer you a cigar."

Wycherly accepted the proffered civility, although the article presented to him was not very promising.

"I have known that young blade," said the stranger, "a matter of ten years or more, and I can honestly say he don't improve upon acquaintance, although I shouldn't hesitate to take his bill if endorsed by the house, as I believe there's money, and they stand A 1 in the City."

"Oh, my business is of a private nature," replied Wycherly. "Nothing to do with money."

"Oh," said the stranger, "then it's something—" he paused for a reply, and receiving none, added, "it's something else."

"Yes, quite so," answered Wycherly. "And if he's the conceited young puppy you say he is, I may have occasion to tell him so."

Their conversation was interrupted by a comic song of a character to make Wycherly rather ashamed of being an auditor, and as the heat of the room, the fumes of tobacco, the badness of the stranger's cigar, combined with other causes which we would rather not particularise, made him more confused and uncomfortable, he announced his intention of retiring.

"I'm with you, sir," said the stranger, and having paid the waiter they ascended the steps leading to the Piazza. The exposure to the air rather increased than diminished Mr. Wycherly's mystification. The stranger therefore offered his arm, and considerately conducted Wycherly to the door of the "Bedford." Some gentlemen, under certain conditions of repletion, are apt to be very open-housed and open-hearted, and Wycherly was one of them. He had arrived at a confused notion that his companion was connected in some way with Hilltown, and being himself very proud of Old Court and hospitable at all times, he formally invited his new friend to pay him a visit during the shooting-season, or fishing-season, or hunting-season, or at any season most convenient to himself, presenting him with a card and receiving another in exchange.

"Well, sir," said the stranger, "I am delighted to have met you, and in this very pleasant way. I hope it may lead to a better understanding between us. I used to hunt and may do so again, and if so Old Court shall see me. As to young Lockyer, take what I have said for what it is worth; but I must ask, now you will know who I am, that you will not give me as the authority for any ill opinion you may form of Master Frank."

"Of course not! of course not!" said Wycherly "I am a gentleman, sir, and you may trust me."

"Not that I care much about it, but we mix up now and then in business and all that. Good-night, Mr. Wycherly, I hope we shall meet often and as friends."

Mr. Wycherly returned this generous sentiment, and after shaking hands with the departing stranger, entered the coffee-room and called for the evening paper. The journal was badly printed, or the news it contained was uninteresting, and Mr. Wycherly therefore soon put it aside and went to bed.

In the morning, when he recalled the events of the past evening, he became curious to learn the name of the person to whom he had been so much indebted, and getting out of bed, referred to the card he had received in exchange for his own respectable pasteboard. It was well for his night's rest that he had deferred the perusal until the morning, as it was inscribed with the name of Mr. J. Selwyn Hartley, Suburban Square.

Wycherly's mortification was extreme. He had only seen Hartley once or twice in former years, and since the death of his old friend Selwyn, he had declined all communication with the fellow, and now to think that he had received and exchanged civilities with him, and under such circumstances, was enough to multiply a hundred-fold the miseries of a sick-headache which was punishing him for his last night's indiscretion.

What use Mr. Hartley made of the adventure we shall learn by-and-by, but at present we must accompany Frank Lockyer on his walk home.

"So Kate Wycherly has judged and condemned me. She has learned, doubtlessly, Ruth's secret, and in the interest of her friend has engaged her father to put me to the question, no doubt of it," thought Frank.

Again, as heretofore, he could not consider his position with Ruth apart from her friend, and Kate's voice was ever in his ear—her estimate of him ever influencing the current of his thoughts. The time had come for definite action; but before he finally committed himself, he would once more seek counsel, judgment perhaps, and abide by it.

Of whom? Cecil?

No; but of his mother—the mother who had loved so tenderly and truly, who had known the terrors of neglected love, and who had pledged him, as it were, beside his father's grave, to do the right, whatever might be sacrificed of self.

His way home was over one of the wooden bridges of the Thames, and it was his custom generally to pause a few moments and linger at night, to watch the water rush past and among the starlings of the bridge before it ran foaming away, a liberated current. The full moon was up, but where the river flowed in the shadow of the bridge, it was made to seem colder and blacker by contrast with the water reflecting the moonlight; and Frank thought on this night, as he had done on many previous ones, how sharp must be the misery, how terrible the despair, which could seek relief in that dark, dismal abyss. As he looked over the railings of the bridge, the sharp cry of a woman's voice and a loud plash in the water beneath startled him, and induced him to believe that some poor wretch had made an end of life, as many, how many! had done before in that merciless river! He hastened towards the spot whence the noise had proceeded, and found that his quick fancy had been too grave in its imagery, and that nothing but a most commonplace incident had occurred, and he smiled at the discovery. A woman had rested her burthen on the rail of the bridge, and it had toppled over into the river. Nothing more. But she had cried out, as her loss would leave her grate fireless for some days to come. Half-a-crown relieved her from that anxiety, and sent her away blessing rather too energetically the donor of the money.

As Frank walked on, however, he could not divest his mind of the first impression it had received when he had heard the scream and the plash in the black, rushing waters, and he thought how often blighted hopes, intolerable remorse, and betrayed love had culminated in such a catastrophe as that which he had imagined to have occurred. Betrayed love! he thought. Love, that was a blessing even in Paradise, and which remains to us as our chief good when valued as the holy thing it should ever be. Oh! woe to him who converts that blessing of our lives into the greatest sorrow! Woe to the betrayer!

Frank paused in his walk to contemplate the phantom he had conjured up.

If he had won Ruth's love, he thought, might she not die without offence to God,—die daily, hourly, from the unconquerable sorrow which he had created thoughtlessly. Gentle, tender Ruth, who had listened to his idle words, and believed them truth! who had remembered looks and tones and acts of kindness, and had given her love in exchange for them! Could he condemn her to the doom of one betrayed? If one must suffer, who should be the victim? His mother should decide.

On the following morning Frank dispatched a message to the City excusing himself from business until the afternoon, and then, when breakfast was ended, solicited his mother's attention to a communication which he desired to make to her. During the night he had thought over the form in which he would present the case to her, fearing that, if he were to inform her how much he was himself interested in her decision, her consideration of justice even might be influenced by her affection for him. He therefore told her that he had been selected by one very dear to him to advise upon a subject of great delicacy and difficulty; and then narrated with the utmost truthfulness the position in which he found himself, and the causes which had led to it. His mother heard him in silence to the end, and her tearful eyes showed him how deeply interested she was in his narration.

"And now, mother," he said, "I ask your counsel. Answer me as though it were your own son who had to decide upon the course of honour and justice, as though it were I who had to choose between the sacrifice of self and the probability of inflicting undeserved suffering on a gentle, loving girl."

Mrs. Lockyer paused for some minutes] before she spoke, and when she did so her voice trembled as though she believed she were really passing sentence on her son.

"Frank," she said, "you have accepted a grave responsibility, almost as grave a duty as a judge who should be called upon to decree life or death, unaided but by the righteous judgment of his own conscience. I think it well that you should have come to me, your loving mother, who would rather see you die than counsel a dishonourable act or decree an unjust sentence. It is well that you have asked me to share the responsibility you have accepted. Be this man, then, who he may—be this girl who she may, provided she be worthy to be loved—there is but one course open which can be acceptable to the Great Judge of all. The love which has been won must be received, and so received that throughout all the years which may follow she who has given it must never feel that it has been taken grudgingly, or without the fullest appreciation of its value. Constant tenderness, watchfulness of every word and act, must supply the absence of that spontaneous devotion which springs from mutual love. If she prove worthy of the sacrifice which has been made, and of those which will have to be made, there may spring up in her husband's heart a gracious feeling which may take the place of love. Man's nature has been created strong that he may bear and find happiness in many things: woman is strong only in her love, and loses all when that is taken from her. The stronger should endure."

Frank was satisfied that his mother had discerned all the truth, and that she had pronounced her judgment knowing that it was he who had incurred the penalty to marry without love.

"You have spoken wisely, justly, and as I believed my own true mother would have spoken," said Frank, as he placed his arms around her, and then kissing her cheeks, glistening with her tears, added, "We will talk again of this, and very shortly, and what more I shall have to say will bring you only comfort."

She could not reply. She could only press him to her bosom, as she had pressed him a thousand times before, when he had had only transient baby griefs which changed to smiles as she embraced him. His greatest sorrow now found comfort from her love.

He went to his own room, and after some hours' reflection wrote two letters,—a brief one to Mr. Wycherly (whose rudeness of the preceding evening he could not forget), excusing himself from calling upon him for the present, and a longer one to Ruth Masham.

The composition of the latter epistle was a work of difficulty, as he had to be watchful of every phrase—every word—in case he should betray the real state of his mind, or awaken even a suspicion in hers that he was not seeking her love spontaneously; and at times he felt as though the very act of writing was in itself a terrible hypocrisy, which sooner or later would revenge itself both upon the deceiver and the deceived.

When he had finished writing he was so little pleased with his production that he tore it into a hundred fragments.

CHAPTER VI.

FRANK LOCKYER'S WOOING BEGINS, AND HE AND CECIL HAVE A LITTLE DINNER ON THE OCCASION—MR. HARTLEY WISHES TO BE A FATHER TO HIS SON.

THE ambassador from Old Court having received his credentials from Mr. Frank Lockyer, returned home forthwith, and gave Kate a faithful account of his clumsily-executed embassy, and neither of them could divine its probable issue. Wycherly became restless and irritable during the succeeding three days, mentally reviling—whenever he looked at Ruth's sorrowful face, or noticed Kate's sympathizing regard of her—Mr. Frank Lockyer as the disturbing cause of their tribulation. Kate was greatly troubled likewise at the ill success of her father's mission, and also by believing that if Ruth should ever learn what had been done in her behalf, the poor stricken girl would feel that she had been unworthily compromised. On the fourth day however the postman left among the family letters at Old Court one addressed to Ruth. Poor child! she knew not what tell-tales her fair cheeks were: how they flushed with hope, and then grew pale with fear, until her mother and her friends would have read the secret of her heart had it not been known to them already.

"A letter for me?" she said, almost breathlessly, and her small white fingers trembled so that she could scarcely remove the envelope which contained the revelation of her destiny.

Mr. Wycherly left the room rapidly, and Mrs. Masham, taking a book, returned to the bay-window.

As Ruth read on she paused more than once to wipe away the mist gathering in her eyes, until she could seen no more, and laid the letter gently upon her lap.

Kate, who had watched her closely, was instantly by her side, as was her mother also.

"What has he written? What has he said?" cried both the conspirators at once. Luckily Ruth heard them not, or she might have wondered why they had guessed so readily that *he* was the writer, and thereby discovered—what she never knew throughout her wedded life—how rude a prompter had given Frank the cue to speak.

Ruth grasped the letter too tightly for her mother to take it from her, or Mrs. Masham would not have hesitated to have satisfied her distressing fears, but when Ruth's consciousness returned, she looked up to her mother's face and smiled so happily, that all her mother's doubts were dispelled, though tears fell rapidly. And then Ruth turned to Kate—her eyes now filled with happy tears also—and held forth the letter.

"Read it, my own dear Kate, read it. I am too happy." Then holding out her arms to her beloved mother, she could only utter, "Come, embrace your happy Ruth," and nestle in her mother's bosom like an affrighted child.

Kate read such tender phrases, such earnest pleading for the heart which had been already given, that the most sensitive of women could not have suspected that Ruth had not been mistress of her own secret, to keep or to reveal as she had elected, and from that time Frank Lockyer won a place in Kate Wycherly's regards from which he could not be displaced even when she was tried sorely.

Love-letters, at the best, are valued only by the hearts, not eyes, which read them, and furnish but matter for a jest when subjected to colder scrutiny. Frank's letter, which had cost him infinite pains so to construct that it should belie the writer, shall remain hidden in the archives of the past, embalmed by the sweetness of the kisses from the lips of Ruth.

The happiness shared by all at Old Court on that evening was remembered in years to come, when unlooked-for changes had made old memories precious.

Ruth could scarcely realize her escape from the terrible forebodings of the past, which had vanished as it were at the touch of an enchanter's wand. Her mother was possessed with a deep thankfulness that Ruth had not wasted her love, but was destined to enjoy its full fruition, whilst Kate, with feelings more akin to those of Ruth, rejoiced as though it had been her own heart which had received the acceptance of its love.

As the ambassador took more than a fair share of credit to himself for this consummation, there was some slight difficulty with Mr. Wycherly now that Mr. Lockyer had made his proposal for Ruth's hand in due and proper form; and by words and winks and frequent innuendoes was more than once on the point of betraying the whole conspiracy. Kate therefore took him to task, and having pointed out the painful consequences which would follow Ruth's suspicion of connivance, so alarmed Mr. Wycherly that he found business in London the next day, and did not come back to Old Court for a week.

When he returned his satisfaction at the state of affairs was not much alloyed by the following letter which he found awaiting him:—

"GRIMES COURT,
"OUT OF GUTTER LANE,
"LONDON.

"DEAR SIR,

"Among the many transactions which I have had with Fortune during a mixed career of commercial and other prosperity and bad seasons, I shall always book my pleasant meeting with you as an event to be placed on the 'profit' side of the balance-sheet. I know that, for some years, our relations towards each other have been, if I may so say, 'soiled' and 'damaged' by misunderstanding upon your part of my method of doing business, and that you have not hesitated to speak of me in terms which conveyed a considerable discount off my respectability. I have therefore kept myself to myself, and though some members of my family [he had written "firm," but had erased the word] have availed themselves of casual introductions to your house, I have waited until your opinions should arrive at maturity, confident that my character would then be duly honoured. I am glad—very glad to know that that time has come; and the kind—the hearty manner I will say in which you met me the other evening at our mutual friend's, Mr. Evans, was such as to wipe out all the remnants as it were of my injured feelings, and bid me hold out the hand of good fellowship as I did at parting, and which you reciprocated in a way which proved your heart to be in the right place. You very kindly invited me to give you a look in at Old Court whenever the pressure of business would permit, and when leisure serves I may do myself that pleasure. My present object in writing to you is not only to cement our reconciliation—as I may call it, but to beg that certain confidences which I made to you respecting F. L.

may be kept *safe* between us, as I find, from consultation with my principal buyer and my accountant, that the party alluded to is of a very violent temper and might consider my remarks made to you as 'private and confidential' an improper interference with his affairs, and it has been suggested he might in consequence forget the difference of years between us, and even have recourse to vulgar personal violence. For my son's sake (more than my own) who is his friend against my will, I would wish to avoid any transaction which would be neither pleasant nor profitable to either. I should be obliged if you will not mention my name in connection with any business you may have in that quarter.

"I will now conclude this long letter by saying ditto to what I have written as to our very pleasant evening, and subscribe myself

"Yours faithfully,

"J. SELWYN HARTLEY."

[To which was added a formidable flourish.]

"P.S.—If you approve the cigar I gave you, I

can let you have some as good as sample at 14s. per hun. duty paid. They are foreign though not warranted from Havannah."

"The cowardly poltroon," thought Wycherly when he had read this letter. "He has maligned the finest hearted fellow I ever knew, and now is afraid of the consequences. I'll set the fellow's mind at rest on that score, at any rate."

And Mr. Wycherly wrote as follows:—

"SIR,

"I am too much ashamed at having been in your company under any circumstances to mention your name to Mr. Frank Lockyer (whom I find to be a thorough gentleman), or anybody else.

"Yours, &c.,

"HERBERT WYCHERLY."

"P.S. I always smoke *tobacco*, in pipe or cigar."

This very rude letter was duly dispatched, but it possibly miscarried, as Mr. Hartley never referred to the receipt of it when he made his own use of the interview and correspondence which caused it to be written.

Since his return from self-exile, Frank and Cecil had not met more than once or twice, as the subject which occupied the thoughts of both when they were together could not be referred to, at least by Cecil, without an apparent intrusiveness—an appearance of pressure, which he had no right to assume. Frank was entitled to form his own opinion of the truth or falsehood of Cecil's surmises from the result of the ordeal to which poor Ruth was subjected; and from that unerring evidence Cecil did not doubt conviction would come to be followed by a noble atonement.

Cecil was very glad therefore to receive a proposal to dine together in a street near Soho Square, at an old tavern, now passed away out of the London Directory, and which then subsisted chiefly on certain memories associated with Goldsmith, Reynolds, and their contemporaries. The coffee-room was large and the tables shone as brightly as bee's-wax could make them, as they had been created before the days when French polish superseded the labour of the housemaid. The proprietor was almost as antiquated as his hostelry, and still clung to a brown wig and silver shoe-buckles. He walked about his deserted coffee-room like a well-preserved host of the last generation, and who had borne with conscious dignity many a bowl of reeking punch to the learned and artistic gentlemen assembled in the Apollo.

Frank had selected this old deserted hostelry as likely to be free from interruption, and Cecil rightly conjectured that some important revelation was in store for him.

When their little dinner was over, and, by special permission of the landlord, they had been permitted to light their cigars in the coffee-room, Frank said—

" Well, Cecil, this seems like old times again;

and I am glad there is to be no longer any reason why our close intimacy should not be at once resumed."

"I have known of no reason why it should have been interrupted, unless——"

"Oh yes, you have," said Frank abruptly; "we have had a shadow between us, old boy, though neither have cared to own it. You remember schooling me once on a time when we drove down to Holly Lodge, little dreaming where that ride was to end; and once again, when your pretty cousin Ruth was in London?"

"Yes," replied Cecil.

"And you concluded on both occasions, as I remember, thus: 'Frank Lockyer, you have trifled and flirted with pretty gentle Ruth, until you have won her liking, and if you disappoint the hopes you have created you are a scoundrel and a scamp."

"No, no! I never said that," replied Cecil.

"But you thought it, and would do so of any other man who had acted as I have done. Say honestly that you would; I wish you to say so."

"Well, I presume there is hardly a choice of terms," said Cecil gravely.

"No, there is not; there is no other name for such a trifler; and if, as I now believe, I have won her maiden love, I am bound by all the laws of honour and honesty to accept it and cherish it 'until death do us part.'"

There was a sort of recklessness in Frank's tone and manner as he said this which for a moment distressed Cecil, and he asked——

"What do you mean?"

"Simply this, Cecil: I am now convinced, not by my own weak vanity or self-esteem, that I have led Ruth to regard me as her lover, and—as you foretold—she has so regarded me, and all her future happiness rests upon the realization of her belief—I have resolved to declare myself what I have appeared to be—her lover."

"And are you not really so? Since you have reflected upon what has passed do you find that you do not love Ruth?" asked Cecil, for he had persuaded himself that Frank had not thought seriously of the state of his own heart, and that when he had done so he would find that Ruth had found her place in it.

"Friend of my youth! Friend of my soul!" said Frank in the same excited tone and manner as he had used from the beginning of this conversation, "I have asked you here to-night to hear my confession: I do not love as I would have desired to love the one I would call my wife, but I have provoked my fate whatever it may be, for good or evil, and will strive from this time forth to endure with cheerfulness."

"My poor Frank!" said Cecil, holding out his hand.

"What!" replied his friend, taking the proffered hand and pressing it firmly. "What! pity me, that am to be the husband of pretty gentle Ruth Masham, into whose eyes I have looked so lovingly, into whose ears I have whispered such loving words that they have reached her heart! To be loved with all her mind, with all her soul, and all her strength! and I will give her in exchange ——" He paused.

"What?" asked Cecil sadly.

"All the tenderness that I can show her; all the honest, honourable devotion of my life. She shall believe that I love her, and be happy —if I can make her so."

"I knew how you would decide, noble old fellow; but I have thought—often since I all but counselled this great sacrifice—should Ruth ever suspect——" Cecil hesitated a moment.

"She never shall, Cecil," replied Frank; "never! You will alone possess the secret of my life—you and my mother; for I felt that to bear what I must bear without your sympathy would have made me disposed to murmur, to repine, and perhaps rebel. Now I can take the path of honour, nor turn back to look regretfully for the road to love which I have missed through my own recklessness."

"But which you may yet find, Frank, and Ruth may show it to you," said Cecil.

"Heaven grant she may, my friend. We will never speak of this matter again, unless——" Frank paused.

"What would you say?" asked Cecil.

"Unless there should come temptation in my way—unless that inexplicable feeling called love should be awakened from its compelled sleep, and I should meet the one whom I could select before all womankind, and yielding as the wise, the good, the brave, have in all ages yielded to the undefined influence, be in danger of revealing the truth to my wedded wife, then, Cecil, I shall come to you to be reminded by your reproaches and your goodness of what my resolves were when I could decide without passion, guided only by my sense of honour and justice."

"May such a time never come," said Cecil earnestly.

"Amen to that prayer," replied Frank, his face flushed and his eyes dilated. "But it may, and—and I may have heard a whisper—No!" he struck his closed hand upon the table, "No! I crush out such a thought and will bring an untouched heart to the marriage altar! . But enough of this ranting. Give me a light, my cigar is out."

The subject uppermost in both their minds was not to be so readily dismissed, so Frank said, after a pause:

"I did not tell you that Mr. Wycherly sent for me the other day, and tried to dragoon me almost into confession. I was annoyed at the time and wondered whether Mrs. Masham had instigated him."

"Certainly not," replied Cecil. "I do not think she suspected the real cause of the change in Ruth. I am sure she did not when they left London."

"I am now satisfied of that also," said Frank; "though the thought got into my mind, and kept back my formal declaration until yesterday."

The two friends were silent for some minutes.

"It is strange," said Frank, "how light words spoken either by oneself or by others are remembered long after, when unlooked-for circumstances give them a value; and I remember you said on our drive to Holly Lodge, 'I shall live to be your best man.' Cecil, I shall claim the fulfilment of that promise when my wedding-day arrives."

Cecil only answered "Yes."

"Yes," repeated Frank, surprised for a moment, and then he added, half jestingly, "Ah! I had forgotten—Kate Wycherly will be bridesmaid, no doubt, and you are afraid of that imperious young lady. Who knows, Cecil, but the interesting event may establish a better understanding between you? I had forgotten for a moment what you said in one of your letters."

"Continue to forget that such nonsense was ever written, Frank," replied Cecil smiling, but colouring deeply. "I don't know how I came to make such a fool of myself, but I fancy that I was wishing to show you that the 'course of true love never did run smooth' with any of us. I can meet Miss Wycherly without any flutter of the heart or annoyance at her disdain, I assure you."

Could he? We doubt it.

"Well, shall we walk?" said Frank. "It is nine o'clock, and I am anxious to see my mother before she goes to bed."

And then the friends (after the Rabelaisean quarter of an hour) went out into the street. They walked on almost in silence, each busied with his own thoughts, in which Ruth and Kate had their full share, until they parted for the night.

When Cecil arrived home he found his father in great good humour,—a somewhat unusual state with him.

"Sit down for a quarter of an hour, Cecil," he said, "and try one of my cigars: not very full flavoured—rather too delicate if they have a fault."

Cecil, although he knew the penalty, accepted his father's civility dutifully.

"Things are very bad in the City," said Hartley, showing his teeth. "I shouldn't be surprised if we have quite a commercial crisis—quite a crisis. I could reckon up half a dozen respectable houses that are very shaky."

"Indeed, sir, that is bad news," said Cecil.

"Bad news?" asked Hartley. "Oh yes, certainly, for those who want money; but what's one man's loss is another man's gain generally, and Bosbury has been overwhelmed to-day by applications for the ready. Some capital bargains, but can't find money for all."

Cecil now understood the cause of his father's hilariousness, and could hardly conceal his disgust.

"I can't understand—for the life of me—how it is—that some people—do not reckonise the great commercial axiom, 'Buy in the cheapest, sell in the dearest market,' said Hartley puffing his cigar or whatever it was he was smoking. "It is the true principle of commerce, and I make it a rule—have made it a rule ever since I took down my shutters—to keep my eye open and watch the turns of the market. Nothing wrong in that I suppose?" and he turned round to show his white teeth to Cecil.

"As a general rule, no, I believe not"—replied Cecil, with some hesitation.

"No—*of course* not—and yet I am quite aware that exception has been taken to our mode of conducting business even by those who ought to have an interest in our success. Perhaps they will think better of it before it is too late. You can have your 2000*l.* to-morrow if you please, or Bosbury shall invest it. No—well, perhaps we had better not mix up matters at present—though as things are very bad in the City and money is in great demand I don't hesitate to say that certain job lots might be bought at—at—well, let us use a common commercial term—a tremendous sacrifice."

Cecil sat silent and Mr. Hartley understood what it implied.

"We live in an age of development," he continued: "a sort of go-a-head era—era?—yes, that's a right word—and amongst other wonderful things young heads know so much better than old ones what is good for their owners. I wish I'd been born twenty years later, and then shouldn't I have been clever! Well, all things come to an end, like that chap," and he threw the end of his cigar into the fender. "And now I'll go to bed.—Candle, Rebecca." And being supplied with one he paused at the door saying, "Oh, by the bye, I didn't tell you, Cecil, or you, mother, that I met old Wycherly the other evening at a friend's of mine?"

Neither Cecil nor his mother could conceal their surprise, and Hartley saw it.

"Really the old fellow was so civil—so anxious apparently to forget and forgive—that I could not have the heart to remember my injuries but shook hands with him like a good Samaritan. There's his card, which he gave me with an invitation to come and see him—which I shall do perhaps when the present commercial crisis is over—if it ever will be this side Christmas. Good night."

Mr. Hartley went to bed very pleased with himself and the adroit manner in which he had introduced his meeting with Mr. Wycherly.

"They 've taken it all in," thought Hartley—"the simple old lady and her clever son—and will believe that Wycherly and me are friends again—that he don't think my business a bar to his friendship; and if that don't bring Master Cecil to my wishes, why, it will mortify him, that 's one comfort."

Mr. Hartley's conscience was as robust as his constitution; and settling his head on his pillow, he fell into a stertorous slumber.

There was Mr. Wycherly's card sure enough, and therefore neither Mrs. Hartley nor Cecil thought the story of the meeting was an invention, although Mr. Wycherly's condonation of the past appeared to be most surprising. With that impression they went to their respective chambers,—Cecil to marvel over the wonderful chance which had reconciled two such opposed men, and to connect with their reconciliation many waking dreams.

CHAPTER VII.

CECIL BEGINS BUSINESS ON HIS OWN ACCOUNT, AND SUCCEEDS IN EFFECTING A FINAL SEPARATION FROM HIS FATHER.

WE have closed for a time our *confessio amoris,* and opened the ledger—a dull volume enough,—and record therein small profit and much loss. Cecil had succeeded, as we know, in obtaining the amount of the debt due in America, and had received half the money as the reward of his success. He had again positively refused to take part in his father's business, preferring to depend upon some New York agency which he had obtained through the influence of Frank Lockyer. When his mother heard of his determination she displayed great emotion, entirely approving of the election he had made, believing, she said, that his honest purpose would prosper, and that he would regard his smaller gains with a satisfaction which would have been otherwise unknown to him. Cecil had been greatly distressed on his return to see how much his mother had changed during his absence. A settled melancholy had taken possession of her, and though she assured him that this would be removed by his society, Cecil rightly conjectured that the knowledge she had obtained from Perks of some wrong-doing of his father—and in which he firmly believed also, although Jim had been reticent whenever the subject had been pressed during their voyage to America—preyed upon her unceasingly. Hartley was not insensible to the alteration in his wife, and attributed it to the strong love she had for her son, and which operated to his own disadvantage; and this conviction acting on such a nature as his, made him more overbearing, captious, and unkind to her and to her daughter Clara, whom Hartley had sent to a cheap boarding-school, resolved, as he said, to have no other child over-educated into learning to despise the man who paid for its schooling. Mrs. Hartley was also conscious of the change in herself, believing that her life was wasting fast, and that death was coming she knew not how, but surely. Still she strove to conceal this presentiment from Cecil, although she had more than once spoken of his sister, and entreated him to regard her as a charge upon his future life.

Cecil had taken a small office in the City, but continued to reside, at his mother's earnest entreaty, in Suburban Square, paying for his board, however, as his father had encouraged him to do, in order "to preserve that independence of which he was so proud, and because he had come to consider the bread on which he had lived all his previous life was much too dirty for a gentleman's eating." The intercourse between father and son was very restricted, all business matters being, as it were by tacit consent, excluded from their conversation.

What great object his father could have in his

perpetual struggle to make money by questionable means Cecil could not conjecture; for although Hartley was mean according to his nature, he was not a niggard in his expenditure whenever his own gratification was to be considered. The pleasure therefore which he derived from gaining and accumulating wealth could only proceed from the innate love of trickery and overreaching which had distinguished him throughout his life. He appeared to be destitute of all natural affection, and evidently regarded Cecil as something which might have been turned commercially to account. For this reason only had Hartley felt any annoyance at the course his son had taken when he refused to be a sharer in his business, and was untouched in any way by the reasons which he had given for selecting an independent position.

Months passed on, and at the beginning of the new year, as the family party sat at table after dinner, Mr. Hartley produced a sheet of foolscap paper, ruled and figured over, and having contemplated it for some time in silence, he threw it towards Cecil, saying—

"That's my balance-sheet; pretty decent tottle, I take it, and somewhat better than yours."

Cecil regarded the paper without much interest, but he saw that the profit on the year had been very considerable.

"How do you think the new firm looks upon paper?" said Hartley, as he threw another sheet towards Cecil, on which was inscribed in Mr. Jones's best round-hand—

"*Selwyn Hartley, Bosbury, Jones, & Co.*"

He repeated the names aloud, and then continued:—"Sounds almost as well as 'Bland & Lockyer' to my mind, and will read quite as well in the Post Office Directory."

"No doubt, sir," replied Cecil, not wishing to provoke any controversy.

"You have sold your mess of porridge, Master Cecil, and these clever fellows have got it a bargain—quite a job lot I may say. They shouldn't have had it so cheap, only they threatened to leave and set up for themselves, which wouldn't suit my book at my time of life, now I've nobody to help me as I ought to have had, thanks to Master Cecil's superfine notions. Well, we shall see: Brag's a good dog, but Holdfast's a better. Mine's not a business for a gentleman I suppose?"

"Is it for an honest man?" asked Cecil, rather imprudently.

"Yes, sir! It is—commercially speaking," replied Hartley sharply, adding after a brief pause: "That's a pretty speech for a son to make to a father, and at his own table. By—I've a great mind to show you the door!"

"He meant nothing unkind, Selwyn," interposed Mrs. Hartley.

"He did, ma'am! He meant to imply that I am not an honest man, and you seem to be of the same opinion if I understand your conduct lately," replied Hartley.

"I am really sorry," said Cecil, "for the words

that escaped me. I certainly do not agree with you, as you know, upon certain matters."

"And what do I care for that, you young puppy?" interrupted Mr. Hartley. "You have chosen your own course, leave me to mine; and I think it will be more agreeable for all parties if Mr. Cecil finds other quarters."

"O Selwyn, do not be so cruel," said Mrs. Hartley, dreading the prospect of separation from Cecil.

"Cruel!—Who's cruel? Not me. Not only does he forget that I'm his father who has spent hundreds on his bringing-up—I can show the account in my ledger—but he insults me in a still more tender part—my character as a man of business. You think me wrong, I've no doubt, and your darling right. If so, you had better pack up and go with him. I dare say I can manage without a wife who is ever whining and sighing, as though her life was a misery to her."

"No, Selwyn," replied Mrs. Hartley in a soft

and broken voice, "I do not desire to forsake my duties to you and to my children. You make those duties hard of performance sometimes, but you are my husband and my children's father."

"Thank you for remembering it," said Hartley; "but now that we are upon the subject, let me be heard once and for all. If Cecil lives in this house he will behave respectfully to me, and you will please to do the same. If he can't, let him pack up as soon as he pleases; and if you can't live without him, pack up too, and I'll make you an allowance. I know what the duties of a father and a husband are, and I am ready to do 'em. I'll have Clara home from school to take care of the keys and keep an eye on the servants. So you can pair off if you like." Having said this, Mr. Hartley walked out of the room, and then into the street, slamming the door after him as though to emphasise his exit speech.

Live with Cecil! Apart from her daily fears and humiliations! Passing the remainder of her life in the peaceful exercise of duties which would be recognised and rewarded by the love of her son! What would not her thankfulness have been for such emancipation! But no—such happiness could not be accepted without violating the vows she had sworn when she became a wife. She had sworn to abide by her husband for "better or worse;" and so she would, until death should dissolve the compact which they had made with each other.

Although Cecil and his mother rarely permitted themselves to discuss Mr. Hartley's conduct or opinions, Cecil was too much pained at what had just occurred to part without saying a few words.

"Mother dear, we have heard to-night how we are valued by the man to whom we ought both to be dear as his heart's blood. No. Perhaps I have deserved little else from him, as I have disapproved the course of nearly his whole life, and rejected what he may have offered in kindness. I have been unfilial, perhaps, in what I have said to him to-night and at other times, and so he may have the right to speak to me as he has done. But you have never offended him except by your virtues and your wifely devotion, and have a claim to be regarded with tenderness and treated with affectionate respect. I cannot endure much longer to be a witness of the humiliation and unkindness to which you are daily subjected, and if I can make a home for you and for my sister, I will remind my father of the disgraceful proceedings of this night, and assert my right to protect you."

"Whatever you may do Cecil—and Heaven I trust will prosper you!—such a conclusion to my life is impossible. I must endure until the end. You love me very dearly—that I know—and would make me happier if you could; and so I ask you, Cecil, to be patient and forgiving where it is your duty to be both."

"I will try, my dear mother," answered Cecil, as he kissed her, and then bade her "Good night."

The next morning Cecil went to his little office with a heavy heart. He opened the two or three letters which made up his "early post," and found among them one from a rough hard-working fellow who had been often seen after business hours and on Sundays loitering about the quays of New York, and looking with rather inflamed eyes at the British ships lying moored there taking in or discharging cargo, he listening to rude English talk, and sometimes joining the conversation as though it were a comfort to hear and to speak his mother tongue to men from the old country. And when some brave ship has sailed out of port, the British ensign flying in the breeze, and known to be on her course to England, that rough labourer has watched her long and earnestly, and turned away at last with a bent head and a heaving bosom. What his thoughts were we may read in his letter to Mr. Cecil Hartley if we care to do so.

"NEW YORK, AMERICA.

"HONOURED SIR,

"i cant stand it no longer hear as i think more and more of old england every day and of old frends though many on them turned there backs on me when i was down. i write, sir, to put you in mine of your promice to me when you was going aboard to come home, and you promiced if i couldnt be happy out hear you would try and get me a plase. pray do, sir, as I shall come home by the next liner as my emploier has got me to work my pasage over. Ples let me find a letter at the agens at Liverpool for me when I land.

"Your obedant servant

"JAMES PERKS."

"Poor Jim!" thought Cecil, "he can't get over his love for the old country. I want a porter, and will try him for the sake of—— What a fool I am!"

Shortly afterwards Frank looked in, as was his daily wont—partly to cheer up Cecil, and partly to report progress as to his wooing. Frank saw that his friend was rather depressed, and naturally inquired the cause; and having heard all that had occurred the preceding night, said:—

"You ought to be used to such scenes by this time, old boy. Why care for such a father?"

"It is because I do *not* care for him that I am unhappy. He is the husband of my mother, who would rather discharge her duties to him though they should kill her than share my home, even if I could offer her one."

"Wait till you have one before you despair of inducing her to quit that—father of yours. You are prospering, are you not?"

"Yes, moderately," replied Cecil. "My capital is too small to admit of any rapid progress, and I often miss advantages for want of means to secure them."

"I wish I could help you, old fellow," said Frank; "but I have to pay for my share in our business out of the profits, so that my allowance is moderate at present. By-and-by I shall have larger means to help you, and even now my private security may serve your turn, and you must use it. My name looks very responsible upon paper, I assure you."

"I do not doubt it, old Frank," replied Cecil, smiling; "but I am not going to bother you in that way. No! no! old friend."

"But yes! yes! old friend," said Frank, smiling also. "Surely our friendship is more than an ordinary acquaintance, and I claim the right to be of use to the risk even of my drachmas. I say with Brutus—you remember when we enacted those noble Romans—

> Shall Francis Lockyer grow so covetous,
> To lock his rascal counters from his friends!

That's not quite the text, but it expresses my meaning."

As there was no necessity for any present demand upon Frank's confidence in his friend, the conversation turned upon Old Court; but Frank continually renewed his offer until certain promising ventures and further advantages in connection with his American agency presented themselves requiring more capital than Cecil had at his command, and Frank would not be denied proving the sincerity of his desire to serve his friend by the dangerous expedient of "lending his name."

In due course of time Captain Calloway of the good ship Curlew, having discharged his cargo and passengers at the Princes' Dock, Liverpool, paid Jim Perks a few shillings over his passage-money and left him to find his way to London the best way he could. When that home-sick vagabond presented himself at the little office in the City, Cecil thought for a moment that the shaggy-whiskered fellow with bronzed throat and chest, and smelling rather powerfully of tar and bilge-water, was apparently more likely to rob a counting-house than take care of one; but having a good opinion of Jim (and so had Kate Wycherly), he did not hesitate to engage him at once as light porter at the munificent honorarium of eighteen shillings a week. Jim was therefore forthwith installed custodian of a complete set of account-books by double entry, certain blotting-pads, rulers, inkstands, copying-press, iron chest, and the ordinary furniture of a counting-house for one; where, having little enough to do in his regular business, Perks employed himself in making mouse-traps on the American principle, varying his work occasionally by manufacturing cabbage-nets, both occupations having stood him in good stead during certain periods of his rambling life. Such events as the engagement of a light porter and his introduction to office seem to be unworthy of record, but they will have much to do —as trifling matters often have—with graver operations, and when sorrow has almost culminated in despair.

The more immediate consequence of Jim Perks' acceptance of office was the effectual estrangement of Cecil and his father, and the completion of a catastrophe which for a time saddened more lives than one.

Cecil had often witnessed exhibitions of his father's distressing ill temper and unreasonable anger, but he had yet to be made acquainted with the fury of a bad man made desperate by his fears.

One day, shortly after the advent of Jim Perks, Cecil returned home to dinner, ana was greatly distressed to find his mother weeping bitterly. There had been a scene evidently, as the tablecloth was thrown upon the carpet, and his father was pacing the room nearly purple in the face from suppressed rage. As soon as Cecil entered the room his angry father confronted him.

"Stay, sir—stay where you are, or I will not answer for the consequences."

Cecil drew himself up, but remembered that it was his father who addressed him.

"I have put up with your infernal insolence, Cecil Hartley, again and again for the sake of appearances, and because that snivelling woman there would have made my home unbearable had I turned you out of the house as I ought to have done." He paused from excess of rage.

"What have I done, sir, to merit this reception?" asked Cecil as coolly as he could.

"What have you done? Dare you ask me that

question, you smooth-faced hypocrite?" And he shook his fist in Cecil's face.

The indignity was hard to bear, but it was a father who offered it to his son.

"I do ask it," said Cecil with effort.

"You do!" screamed Hartley, more enraged by Cecil's coolness, "—— you! You and your precious mother, when I was toiling like a galley-slave to make the money you spent like water, took advantage of your stay at Hilltown to hunt up old scandals—old devilish lies that were told to crush me once and to cheat me out of my birthright. You took a pleasure in making out your father to be a scoundrel, if not something worse—a felon almost; and if you had gathered proofs enough to have hung me, you would have done it, perhaps, if it had served your purpose."

"I will not hear this wicked raving longer," said Cecil. "You are mad, sir!"

"Mad! No; I am sane and sound, as you shall find when my will is read to you, ungrateful scamp!" cried Hartley, speaking at the top of his voice. "What are you colleaguing together to do—you and the Mashams, I suppose? But I defy you and your witness and all the lot of you!"

"If you will make yourself understood I may be able to answer you," said Cecil. "At present I can only wonder at your meaning."

"Indeed, sir! Indeed, sir!" replied Hartley, advancing his face close to that of Cecil. "You lie, sir, when you say you do not understand me. But I will speak plainer, and ask you what right have you—my son, worse luck—to employ as your confidential servant a man who has dared to threaten me with—with I don't know what—who has extorted money from me again and again, and who is ready to swear my character away if anybody will pay him to do so?"

"If you mean that by engaging James Perks——"

"That is what I do mean, and you knew it. You have mixed yourself up with all your father's oldest, bitterest enemies—the Mashams, the

Wycherlys; and now, to crown all, you take into your pay this Jim Perks, who—who ought to have died in a ditch for what he has done to me."

"I know of nothing which the man has done except to have acquired a bad name when in England before, from causes I would rather not particularise," said Cecil, losing control over himself.

"But you shall 'particularise,' as you call it, my fine gentleman," replied Hartley, again thrusting his face offensively forward. "I insist upon knowing what you mean by your big words, sir."

Cecil went to his mother, and taking her by the hand led her, unresisting, from the room.

"Now, sir," said Hartley, folding his arms, and standing as it were at bay—"out with it."

"This has been said of that man,—and remember that you have demanded it of me."

"I do demand it," said Hartley, stamping his foot and compressing his lips together. "Now, sir, speak out. What has been said?"

"That you have used this man as your tool; that when your uncle Selwyn died this man's name was attached as witness to a will——" Cecil paused.

"Well!" said Hartley, "that's no news! that was plain enough, and none dared dispute it."

"No; but though that was the will your uncle Selwyn signed, men—mind *I* do not say this—men do not hesitate to say that some juggle had been practised, and that this James Perks could have disclosed it had he been so minded."

"Is that all, sir, that men say and which you have listened to and not knocked the speaker down?" asked Hartley.

"No, sir, it is not all. They say that you lent colour to these suspicions by giving this man money, which he spent, as ill-gotten money is usually wasted, in riot and drink, until he could trade upon your fears no longer, and then you left him to starve or to steal—drove him to gaol and to desperation almost."

"And who deserved it more than he did, a

cursed extortionate thief!" cried Hartley. "And this is the man that you take into your office, as though you would publish to the world—the commercial world particularly—'Here, gentlemen, this is the fellow my father kicked out of doors because he grew tired of being robbed of his money to keep his lying tongue quiet; and when I grew desperate at last, I let him say his worst, and had lived it down until you, my son—my only son—ripped up the old story and set men's tongues wagging again."

"Your conscience is accusing you, sir," said Cecil.

"I have no conscience that accuses me!" replied Hartley fiercely; "and that being the case I will have no son to take its place. Leave this house at once—your things shall be sent after you; but from this hour you and I, Cecil Hartley, are two—no more to each other than if we had never seen each other. If you were standing beneath a gallows and I could save you from the rope I wouldn't do it!"

And the oath he swore when he had said this, he kept to the full when the time came in which he remembered it.

Cecil left the house without attempting to see his mother, as he feared that had he done so the angry devil which then had possession of his father might be provoked to greater cruelty towards her when he was gone. But for her, Cecil would have rejoiced to have had this final separation from the man whose blood flowed in his veins, but whose wickedness was repugnant to his nature.

CHAPTER VIII.

FRANK'S WOOING TERMINATES IN MATRIMONY—HIS BEST MAN IS MADE BOTH SAD AND HAPPY.

WINTER has come and gone when we resume our story. We have passed over the intervening time, as we intend to summarise the incidents which have taken place, and not because we would show any disrespect to winter, which has much to commend it, especially when met in the country. A clear frosty day braces the nerves and provokes to exercise, whilst it gives new charms to every landscape, powdering, as it were, the trees and hedgerows and grassy fields with pearls and diamonds, or when the snow has fallen changes all around into a fantastic newness, bringing at least to us a feeling of solemn peacefulness. Within doors the fire burns brighter, and draws around it the household faces we love the most, perhaps to come back to us in after years, associated with the pleasant converse of those winter gatherings, replacing the gaps which death and change will make in every social circle. The pleasant rubber, a game at chess, the hit at backgammon, and the noisy, merry, round game, have double interest when played on winter nights, and help to make up the memories of home—the dearest of all memories. Winter brings Christmas time, and though it is somewhat the fashion now-a-days to scoff at that goodly season, we of the old world welcome its coming and love its social customs dearly, believing that—remembering the great event it commemorates—many recall also the duty of forgiveness and the necessity for charity. We confess to an earnest detestation of choking fogs and greasy streets, lodging-house fires, damp cabs and stumbling horses, sooted snow and miserable thaws, pertaining to London city; but we can also recall glowing faces passing in the streets, and many a happy meeting of congenial friends whom winter brought together. Spring, summer, autumn, show some "trail of the serpent," and winter is not exempt from the general doom. Hunger is doubly keen, sickness more poignant, shelter more needful, when winter is abroad; but good men and women can then do God's work unsparingly, and discharge those duties for which health and ease and wealth were given them in trust for others. Enviable privilege!—Grave responsibility!

Winter has gone, and so let us sing with the poet of Youth and Love, Thomas Moore:—

> "Of all the gay months which round the sun
> In gay wreathed dance their courses run,
> Sweet May! sweet May the month for me!"

and hastening down to Old Court, learn how the last few months have been spent by those in whom we have an interest.

A more constant wooer than Frank could not be, and gentle Ruth was happy. She had paid more than one long visit to Mrs. Lockyer, and had been already adopted as a daughter—so completely had her gentleness and goodness won upon that lady, and Frank often wondered why his own regard would not grow into love also. Perhaps it might have done had he not worn the rosy chain of Hymen by compulsion; but there were thorns among the roses which surrounded his golden fetter,—if it be not a libel on the holy state thus to designate a wedding-ring. There might have been another cause; but as he would not admit it, even to himself, we will be silent also.

For Ruth's sake Mrs. Lockyer had striven very hard with old prejudices, and always endeavoured to receive Mrs. Masham as though the Rosebush had been some old ancestral tree having root in a Norman baron, and not the sign of a modest public-house. It was rather difficult to maintain the illusion even when Mrs. Lockyer visited Old Court, where the Mashams now resided whenever they were in the country, as their presence made the old moated house almost as pleasant a place as it was before it became ghost-haunted to Wycherly. He had, apparently, long since put aside all sorrow for his dead wife; but whenever there were pleasant, happy hours within the walls of Old Court she was by his side, a welcome visitant unknown to all but him, dividing yet increasing his share of the passing enjoyment.

Cecil Hartley was also a frequent guest, as the quarrel with his father had given Mr. Wycherly a more favourable opinion of the young man; a circumstance which surprised Cecil at first, when he remembered the reconciliation which had taken place between the two ancient foes—according to Mr. Selwyn Hartley's representation. That wicked old huckster had intended, as we have seen, to have used the fortuitous meeting with Mr. Wycherly to mortify his son, and possibly, by assuming to be on friendly terms with such a man, weaken Cecil's objection to the job-lot business. As the interview was never alluded to by either Wycherly or Cecil, its real character remained unexplained until it had acquired an influence in a direction which was never contemplated by the malicious narrator.

Cecil was prospering in his business fairly but slowly, assisted frequently by the kindness of Frank Lockyer, whose confidence in his friend appeared to be unlimited. His mother visited him at stated intervals appointed by Mr. Hartley, usually remaining with him for a day or two, and always striving to appear happier than he had hitherto known her. Was she acting a part which was exhausting the little life remaining to her in order to deceive her devoted son? Cecil suspected nothing, and would therefore have been comparatively happy but for the increasing love he had for Kate Wycherly, and which sometimes he believed to be utterly hopeless, as the change in Mr. Wycherly's reception of him had produced none in the one whose good opinion he coveted so earnestly. She never displayed more than the most ordinary interest, and received him with as much reserve as good breeding and her own kind nature permitted. True, she was the same to all the eligible young gentlemen who occasionally visited Wycherly at Old Court, and she made no secret of her determination to devote her entire affection to supply in part the place left vacant by her mother. Cecil knew he had no rival, and such consolation as that reflection could bring him he had to revive his hopes when they had almost died within his heart.

Thus matters stood one bright May day. Frank and Cecil were on a visit at Old Court, and Ruth expressed—as she had frequently done before—her great desire to visit her uncle Jerry, whom she had never seen since he left Hilltown, and who had refused all Mr. Wycherly's invitations to spend some of his infrequent holidays with them. It was therefore arranged that Frank should write to Mr. Garrett and invite him to dine with him and a friend or two at the inn where they had passed the evening together; and that as Mr. Wycherly was kind enough to place his horses at their disposal, they should drive to Beckbury—some fifteen miles from Old Court—and return in the evening. Kate, "as usual," Cecil said, excused herself from being of the party, and Mrs. Masham would have done so, had not Frank insisted that she should go with him, finding a malicious pleasure in anticipating the meeting between the old sweethearts.

As love-making is very dull work for those who are lookers-on, and not less uninteresting when coldly described by any one less interested than the lovers themselves, we will leave untold the tender nothings with which Frank continued to fill the ear of his loving Ruth, and receive the little party at the door of the inn at Beckbury.

Mrs. Masham had been very fidgety and abstracted at times during the morning, and there was a certain excitement in her manner which amused Frank, who alone conjectured the cause. In due time Jerry (we must call him Jerry, please) arrived, evidently arranged at his very best, his well-inked hair smoothly brushed and shining.

Frank having watched for his arrival, received him very heartily, and then proceeded to introduce him to the rest of the party. Jerry was rather taken aback at the presence of ladies, but soon recovered his old manner when performing behind his counter at Hilltown.

"This lady is your niece, Mr. Garrett," said Frank, "Ruth Masham;" and before Jerry could recover from his surprise, pretty Ruth had kissed his old cheek and changed its wrinkles into smiles.

"And this lady perhaps needs no introduction," continued Frank: "Mrs. Masham, your sister-in-law." At this announcement the wrinkles abolished the smiles, until Mrs. Masham shook him heartily by the hand, and declared her great pleasure in meeting her old friend once more. Women disguise their feelings so much better than men. Perhaps it is a necessity of their social condition which compels them to conceal what they would more willingly confess; but if Mrs. Masham had had Jerry in her mind, and had thought of him in connection with their old relations towards each other, no one would have suspected it from the easy way in which she trotted poor Jerry over his memories of the past, and twitted him with his withdrawal from his old friends and relations.

Jerry stumbled a good deal as he attempted to follow cousin Hester—she insisted upon being called so—and would fairly have broken down had not the others come to his rescue. It was a wonder that even the custard pudding had not choked him, so spasmodically did he swallow his dinner. But the good wine which had been brought from Old Court put heart into the poor schoolmaster, and what at one time promised to be a very embarrassing meeting proved to be a most agreeable one.

"You asked me just now," said Jerry, shaking the inky side of his head at Mrs. Masham, "what made me run away from Hilltown? Would you believe, Ruth dear, would you believe, gentlemen, it was that lady's cruelty; and a very good thing for her that she did so! I should have made a very bad husband, don't you think so, Cousin Hester?"

Ruth, maiden Ruth, could not have blushed redder than did her veteran mother at this appeal, and to which, for the life of her, she could only reply, "What nonsense you are talking, Jerry."

Jerry did not care to pursue the flying, and so he turned to Cecil,—

"And you are the son of Mr. Jacob Selwyn Hartley, sir. I am glad to see you with these friends of mine to-day, because it assures me that you are worthy to be respected by good people. Let us take a glass together to drown any old grudge I may have to one of your name, and to wish for better acquaintance with each other." That libation was to be remembered in years to come.

When dinner was over, Ruth requested permission to visit the school-house, as she had passed some anxious—some happy hours in such a place, "and should like to think," she said, "of Uncle Jerry now and then, as he would be engaged in the discharge of duties which were becoming every day, to be considered more honourable."

Jerry was pleased at Ruth's remark, and led the way forthwith to his little school-house, assuming a mock gravity as he introduced his friends to his rough desks and forms and ink-bespattered walls.

"The respect which you say, Ruth, is to be accorded to the educator of the young has not yet reached Beckbury, you see, by the accommodation accorded to myself and pupils. This is my schoolroom; yonder is my 'parlour, kitchen, and hall,' to which you are all heartily welcome," said Jerry.

Thereupon Mrs. Masham and Cecil entered Jerry's little room, which was quite filled by the assembled company.

"It is very tidily kept," remarked Mrs. Masham; "and no doubt——" but she paused as her eye fell upon the portrait of a lady which, despite its very defective execution and unfavourable resemblance, she at once suspected to be intended for herself. Her hair, before Time had touched it very tenderly, was something of that colour. She had—long years ago—once worn a muslin dress dotted over with purple stars, and there was a little mole upon the painted face which had its counterpart upon her own. "What a silly, foolish fellow Jerry Garrett was!"

As Ruth and Frank accompanied by their host entered the little room, Mrs. Masham went to the window, where upon a small table lay a Bible covered with green baize. Why she raised its cover she knew not, for she guessed the book it was; but having done so, she saw, carefully pasted within it, a piece of paper on which was figured two turtle-doves holding a true lover's knot, and beneath it four jingling lines were written which she remembered to have heard and to have transcribed twenty-three years ago! "What a place to keep an old valentine," thought Hester Masham, as she closed the book and walked quietly into the dirty schoolroom. Jerry's *lares* were few in number, and he certainly kept them in odd places.

The school-house was once more abandoned to its solitude, and the party strolled back to the inn. After exacting a promise from Jerry to accept Mr. Wycherly's next invitation — Mrs. Masham taking no part in the solicitation—the poor schoolmaster watched the dust of the departing wheels bearing away, one at least, whom he had never expected to have seen under the roof of his humble home.

As Cecil rode on the box with the driver, Mrs. Masham very properly closed her eyes, and went, if not to sleep, into the land of dreams, and saw many visions of the past, and one confused and improbable phantasm of the future. She also thought, amongst other thoughts, that in a short time Ruth would be married, and then she could no longer remain as she had done at Old Court, but must seek a lonely home among strangers, perhaps, away from Hilltown.

The sole object of her later life, for which she had struggled with sorrows and toiled late and early, was about to be accomplished, and Ruth was to be made happy, though in another home than hers, and with a younger guardian, who would demand in exchange for his care and devotion all her companionship and watchful love. Hester never believed that her child would forget what was due to her, the devoted mother, or cease to abound in filial gratitude for the tender recollections of the past; but she knew that there was to be a new life for Ruth, and wherein she must hold a second place. Yet she rejoiced that the time was near at hand when the fears which had possessed her again and again, that Ruth would be alone should death remove her mother, were to have an end, and that there was another bosom to share her sorrows and to strive for her happiness with an untiring patience. What care then for herself? If there were no one to love her but Ruth;—and then that dingy school-room and its narrow parlour—the rude effigy, the baize-covered Bible, and the faded valentine—came into her waking dream, and with an angry shrug she roused herself to see the head of her pretty Ruth resting fondly on the shoulder of her affianced husband.

Jerry Garrett was a silly old fellow, and from that time forth Mrs. Hester Masham resolved never to think of him for more than a moment at a time.

The courtship of Ruth and Frank has been a very long one, patient reader, and now, so please you, we will "Haste to the wedding."

Ruth's nineteenth birthday was close at hand, and on that anniversary she was to be married. Mr. Wycherly claimed to act *in loco parentis*, and to have the honour of giving the wedding breakfast at Old Court; and as many friends as the bay-windowed dining-room would inconveniently hold were invited. Mr. Frank Lockyer departed for Old Court, after Cecil had gladly accepted the office of best-man to redeem a promise given, when none could have foreseen how that day's ride was to be the beginning of a journey that was to end but with the lives of many.

A cloudless day, a merry gathering, and away to church, and none believed who stood around the altar that the blessing of the priest had not joined two hearts as well as hands together. Frank's calm and tender manner convinced even his mother and Cecil that the bridegroom had loved at last, and married where he loved. Yet there were cold drops upon his forehead, and his tongue dried and his lips whitened as he uttered the words which bound him to his bride, and when he knelt beside her he prayed earnestly to be strengthened to keep the vows he had sworn until his life's end, never to falter in his duty to her, but through all the years allotted to him to act as though he loved as she believed he did. With a strong will he drove all depressing thoughts away, and when he led his wife—his Ruth—through the crowd of eyes in the church and beside the path leading from it, none saw a trace of sorrow in his face, and all went "merry as their marriage bells."

Uncle Jerry had been compelled to come to the wedding, as a new suit of pepper-and-salt had been made on speculation by Mr. Wycherly's order, and sent over by a groom with strict orders not to return without Mr. Garrett. Accordingly he duly arrived, but no persuasion whatever could get him to the church. He volunteered however to assist the parish schoolmaster in marshalling the boys and acting as fugleman when the cheering was to take place; but unluckily he became so agitated, that under his misdirection the lads gave three cheers for the beadle, whom they detested; and as Jerry insisted upon making the boys reparation by a liberal distribution of sweets, they were discovered to have their mouths filled with brandy-balls when the proper moment arrived for cheering the happy pair, and many of them nearly suffocated themselves in discharging their duty of huzzaing everybody.

It is not our purpose to record the eloquence

of the breakfast-table, applauded as it was to the demolition of wine-glasses and other fragile accessories. Enough that Mr. Wycherly started off at score; but, to quote the Master of the Hilltown Hounds, he came a cropper at his third fence (or sentence), but having picked himself up with remarkable cleverness, rammed himself at a double compliment, and finished beautifully. The parson —a general favourite—spoke greatly to the purpose when proposing the health of Mr. Wycherly, but was thought to have been rather indiscreet when he spoke of him as Ruth's father-in-law. The Hilltown lawyer, being young and unattached, was permitted to propose the bridesmaids, and was considered to be exceedingly liberal when he promised to draw up their marriage settlements for costs out of pocket. And Cecil, as best-man, being compelled to return thanks, would have been eminently successful had not his eyes met those of Kate Wycherly, then regarding him as though whatever prejudice she had was positively in his favour. The surprise overpowered him, and he arrived at rather an untimely end.

The happy pair were to have a three months' holiday to rove over the map of Europe nearly, and therefore the kissing at parting was more than usually abundant, and the luggage more prolific than accommodating. All was arranged at last—the last box stowed in its place, the last kiss and the last hand-shake given, the old shoe thrown, and then the happy pair departed.

As Cecil watched the carriage disappear he felt—he knew not why—that some terrible evil was to be connected with Frank's departure, and that they should never meet again as they had met, being separated by some overwhelming sorrow. Poor fellow! Was the feeling to be prophetic?

Cecil turned into a side-path in the garden—the same which Mrs. Masham had taken when she made the discovery of Ruth's great secret—and as he approached the summer-house he thought he heard sobs, as though some one was in grief within it. As he drew nearer a voice broken by tears, prayed that strength might be given to overcome the selfish feeling that was tempting to the forgetfulness of duty, and implored God's blessing on the election which had been made for a future life. Cecil knew the voice, and thought he understood the prayer. He would have retreated unobserved, but before he could do so Kate Wycherly came from the summer-house, her eyes red from weeping. She saw Cecil instantly, and clasping her hands together, exclaimed, "You here, Cecil Hartley!" and then covering her eyes for a moment, fled as though from some evil influence.

Fatigue, indisposition, were pleaded for her absence for the rest of the evening. When she met Cecil in the morning he hesitated to approach her as they were alone, but holding out both her hands to him, she said—her voice like sweetest music—"Forgive my strange conduct to you yesterday, Cecil Hartley!"

What could he do but press her hand to his lips for the first time, and the last perhaps.

Kate drew away her hand; but when Cecil looked into her face for pardon, a smile was fading from her lips, and there was no anger in her eyes.

How often would that face come back to him blending with his dreams when he was most happy; passing also before him in his waking hours, and leaving him more wretched from the remembrance of all that he had lost!

CHAPTER IX.

QUITE A BUSINESS CHAPTER.—CECIL STARTS ON THE ROAD TO RUIN.

THE excitement and bustle which usually precedes a wedding had not been wanting at Old Court, and though Mrs. Masham would at times refer to her own anticipated loneliness when Ruth should have left them, none conjectured how much the loss of her companionship would be felt by her who had been so constant in her friendship—Kate Wycherly. It was in vain that that true-hearted girl strove to conceal from Mr. Wycherly that some change had come over her pleasant life, and that her mind was possessed with graver thoughts than she had known hitherto. She strove to smile as gaily as she had been wont to do when Ruth was with her, to sing as blithely and to walk with as lithe a step. But her father watched her with his heart, and saw that a change had come, and in his wisdom ascribed it to the loss of Ruth. At length he began to chide her for such foolish regrets, which were at first disclaimed, but after a more earnest remonstrance than usual, Kate said to him,—

"You must not watch or question me so closely, dear papa, or I shall learn to be afraid of you. You loved Ruth, and miss her greatly, do you not? Yet you cannot know the friend whom I have lost; one whose noble nature can never be excelled, and with whom I could have passed my life had Heaven so willed it. I did not know all this until the day Ruth left us, and as I had determined long ago that you should have no rival in my love—not even Ruth—I have struggled with and will subdue this uninvited intruder if you will leave me to myself. And you will do so, papa, and from this time you will let me be a little solemn when I please, and as becomes me at twenty-two!"

Wycherly could only say that "she was a strange girl—a good girl to care so much for Ruth," as there was that in her voice and face which made her words seem like a command.

A month after the wedding, and Kate had not improved, and therefore Mr. Wycherly took counsel with Mrs. Masham, and another little tour on the Continent was arranged, Mrs. Masham gratefully agreeing to be of the party. Kate was delighted with this proposal, and the business of packing and preparing seemed to dispel much of the tristness which had possessed her of late, and Wycherly was happy again.

Cecil had returned to his business, and found it to possess an interest which he had never known before. "Mr. Wycherly's prejudice against me is gone, although he has never mentioned to me his reconciliation with Mr. Hartley; and Kate, proud darling Kate, is at least as forgiving as her father. Who knows what time may do?"

Ah! who knows!

One evening shortly after, he found his mother

at his lodgings. She rose to receive him, and when they had embraced, as was their invariable custom, she said with a sad smile, "Cecil dear, what I have resisted so long has come at last. You know how patiently I have borne the hard life your father elected should be mine; but to-day—to-day, he has insisted that I should carry myself where I have left my love and duty, and ask you for a home."

"Mother dear!——"

"Yes, Cecil, ever since you have left us such has been my daily taunt; but I remembered my duty as a wife, and bore in silence. To-day he has interpreted my submission as 'insufferable insolence,' and I am here to ask you for a home."

"The greatest kindness he has ever done us," cried Cecil, his eyes sparkling with resentment,—"and my sister?"

"Is to remain at school, although I am permitted to visit her when I please, and to have her with me during holidays,"—and "snivel over her," Mr. Hartley had added.

"That's better than I hoped for," said Cecil, all his resentment gone—lost in the pleasurable thought that his mother was at last free from the domestic tyranny which had oppressed her for so many years. "I am so proud, so happy, at this new change, that I can hardly contain myself. It could not have come at a better time; there are rooms I know vacant here, and by-and-by we will have a little house of our own, and make a home at last!"

Very reluctantly Mrs. Hartley was made to tell her son of the cowardly persecutions which she had endured from her husband; and though he had not used any personal violence, his brutal language—far more brutal than any which we have recorded—had bruised her heart.

In a few days Mrs. Hartley was quietly settled in her new home, and Cecil pictured to himself a pleasant future in which his mother and —had his hopes become so bold?—Kate Wycherly were portrayed. Strange, that the presentiment of evil which had possessed him when Frank departed from Old Court did not return; no, not even when he remembered how much the future of his fancy depended for its realisation on the chances of fortune. Could he have foreseen what a week would bring, how different would have been the picture!

The American mail had been looked for with some anxiety by Cecil, as he was expecting to receive by it a remittance of considerable amount, and which was already anticipated to pay an acceptance for 500*l.* given him by Frank Lockyer. He was delighted therefore to receive the expected letter, although the superscription was not in the handwriting of his correspondent. He opened it and read his utter ruin, although he knew it not at that moment. The letter was from a stranger to Cecil, but from its legal phraseology, not to be misunderstood, he learned that his debtor was irretrievably beggared, and all chance of future payment hopeless. The loss of so much money would have been distressing enough, but not ruin had it come when Frank was in England; but now, without the means of raising a fourth of the sum required to meet the bill due in three days, the consequences were fearful indeed! All his means were locked up in other American ventures, and he had no credit in the usual channels for raising money. To dishonour the bill would be to damage the commercial reputation—more sensitive of injury almost than the fair fame of woman—of himself—of Frank! Frank, the friend who had trusted so implicitly to his honour! Cecil was nearly stunned by these reflections, and knew not what to do. Should he apply to Frank's partner? He knew that would produce only discord between them, as the older and more cautious trader had warned both Frank and Cecil of the danger they were incurring, and partly exacted their promise, to abandon such unbusiness-like transactions. No, that door was closed, and he could think of no other, except to go to the holder of the bill and explain his difficulties.

The man who had discounted the bill lived in

one of the faded squares of London, and had grown rich by usury; and all pertaining to his house gave evidence of the multifariousness of his dealings. The room into which Cecil was shown had been, and perhaps was then, a dining-room; but now the dingy hangings of rich brocade—some spendthrift's purchase, the sooty Turkey carpet "of noble dimensions," the faded morocco chairs and tomb-like sideboard, proclaimed that men were eaten there—needy fathers, thoughtless sons, struggling traders. The ogre himself sat in an adjoining room, in which choice *bijouterie* was liberally displayed. An elegant writing-table with a silver inkstand was the altar of sacrifice; and the sacrificial priest, arrayed in a furred dressing-gown (although it was summer), played with an ivory paper-knife, as though there could be no danger in approaching him. There was a forced smile upon the fellow's face as Cecil entered, but the greed of gain instantly dispelled it, and left the upper lip ruled as it were with the lines of a ledger. There was no hope of any sympathy from him, and Cecil sighed heavily when his request for time was curtly refused.

"Pay the bill, and I'll see then what can be done, perhaps, sir," was the sentence of this modern Gripeall.

There are kindly, honest men who deal in money and sell it at a fair and marketable usance, and who look upon such a vampire as held poor Cecil in thrall as a criminal whom the law cannot touch without infringing on the "Liberty of the Subject,"—that constitutional safeguard for some of the dirtiest rogues in the community.

Poor Cecil wandered back to the City, taking by-streets as though he feared to have his misfortune read in his face, and found that his inexorable debtor had already sent a note to await his return. It was only two lines, but they were of terrible import to Cecil.

"SIR,

"I think it right to inform you that if

there is any irregularity with Mr. Lockyer's bill for 500*l.*, I shall proceed instantly.

"Yours obediently,

"JOSEPH SKINNER."

So—that was plain enough.

It was late before Cecil reached his lodgings that night, as he wished to avoid seeing his mother, and she had retired to rest unconscious, happily, for that night at least, of the horrible devil Cecil had brought with him into the house, to sit with him throughout the greater part of the night, and then to lie beside his pillow, crying incessantly, "Ruin! Ruin! to him who trusted you! Ruin to all you hoped for and believed was in your future!"

No doubt of it. Frank's fair fame would suffer greatly; and Cecil would have been wiser had he gone to Mr. Bland, the stern hard-headed partner. He was afraid of compromising Frank, and obtaining no assistance by the appeal. Ruin to himself! Yes; and what did that involve? Leaving his mother at the mercy of her brutal husband, who would make her son's misfortune the theme for his bitter sneers, his cruel jibes, his savage irony, until her heart broke, perhaps, being too full of misery. What else?

O the abandonment of those sweet hopes which had just had birth! The hope that Kate might love him! The hope that, when his toil had been successful and he had made a home, he could have asked her to have shared it with him! Miserable reverse! Bankrupt! Disgraced by failure and betrayal of his friend, she—even if he had understood her words, her look aright—she would expel him from her heart, and only remember him associated with dishonour!

The night passed at last, and when Cecil met his mother she instantly perceived that some great trouble had overtaken her son. Cecil was a bad dissembler, and knowing how much the result of the present difficulty was likely to affect his mother, he told her how desperate was his position, and how vainly he had tried to escape from it. She heard him with deep sympathy, but could find no words of comfort, none seemingly of counsel.

When Cecil had left the house for the City, scarcely less dreadful to him than it was to those who once heard the cry, "Bring out your dead," resounding in its streets, Mrs. Hartley wrote an earnest appeal to her husband, disclosing Cecil's requirements and asking for assistance.

"So that's what it's come to," wrote Mr. Hartley in reply. "Burst up in less than a twelvemonth. Ruined for 500*l.*!—Kite-flying's a dangerous game, and requires a very long string to make it pleasant. And you ask me to lend our darling son the money he wants. What son is he to me? No more than the King of the Sandwich Islands. He has insulted me in my own house, at my own table, my own mahogany, which is a sacred thing, or ought to be. No, madam, my money's too dirty for his handling, even with kid-gloves on; my way of keeping shop open isn't wholesale enough for such a commercial gentleman as he wanted to be! Let him go to them as he considers his equals, and not come to a poor, pettifogging common man like his unworthy father. I repeat it again, madam, and you may tell him so, my money's too dirty for him to touch, and if it would save him from worse than Basinghall Street, I wouldn't draw a cheque for one-pound-one. All I shall say is this, if you like to come home again you can. You can have the keys again whenever you like, but then—you give up the gent 'on the verge of ruin,' and stick to your duty as the wife of

"Yours, &c.,

"J. SELWYN HARTLEY."

Mrs. Hartley was at first inclined to keep this letter from the knowledge of Cecil, but upon reflection, she thought it better to let him know what she had done in his behalf, and how utterly hopeless was her expectancy of assistance from his father.

The position was becoming desperate! Every day, every hour brought near the catastrophe of ruin! The first reflections which had come to Cecil returned with every hour almost, until his brain grew confused and he could be hardly considered master of his words or actions.

He talked aloud, turned over and over again the book of accounts, and figured calculations which were incapable of realisation. At last he went to Mr. Bland, Frank's partner. He had gone into Scotland to attend the deathbed of his only brother. No hope there, as in two days more the bill would be due for payment. He wandered about, not daring to go home, not capable of remaining in his office, where Jim Perks sat wondering what had happened, so to disturb his kind young master.

"If Frank Lockyer had been in England, all would have been well," thought Cecil. "Ah! I remember well the presentiment of some coming sorrow which possessed me when he went away. If I could have written to him—if I could have procured——;" he staggered and clung to the railing of the Park, where he was walking, or sauntering rather. What suggestion had seized upon his mind? What streak of light glimmered through the darkness, showing him also pitfalls and hideous things to scare him back. "Ruin! ruin to friend and self! Ruin to hope and love!" resounded in his ears; and there was a way to avoid the threatened evil if he dare take it. Why did he hesitate? There was a dreadful penalty if he failed to accomplish it; and yet no moral wrong, he thought, stood in the way! Wrong to none! safety to him and others! His limbs trembled, and large drops of cold sweat fell from his hair and forehead, as though an agony had taken possession of him. His face was so changed, so deeply lined and rigid, that many who knew him would have passed him by as one unknown to them. After a time he appeared to recover from the first great shock of this new idea, and yet he stopped in his walk and looked upon the ground, never caring to raise his eyes to heaven.

When he reached home he tried to amuse his mother with idle talk and boyish recollections, anecdotes of his school days, and what great plans he and Frank had formed, none of which had interest for them now, and then pleading fatigue bade her "good-night," pausing at the door to say, "I forgot to tell you, I believe all will yet be right in the City. Good-night again."

He slept soundly. He had scarcely closed his eyes for two nights before; but either his brain could bear no longer or he had found some certain succour, and sleep came.

Cecil walked to the City in the morning like one who had no interest in the busy world around him, neither looking to the right nor to the left, and scarcely pausing when he had to cross a street, occasionally provoking the expletives of the excitable drivers of the passing vehicles, and so he continued until he reached his office in the City. He scarcely noticed Jim Perks, but went at once into his private room and closed the door after him. There was much deliberation in all he did.

He brushed his hat before he hung it upon its peg, carefully smoothed his gloves, appearing to delay the accomplishment of some object as long as possible. He then unlocked his desk and opened it. The first thing which met his eye was Mr. Skinner's warning letter, and having read it he threw it into a corner of his desk. From one of the pigeon-holes he took a packet of letters from Frank Lockyer and examined them carefully, selecting at length one, which had only reference to some trifling matter of business, and was dated from the office. This he placed upon the desk and studied it with more attention than the matter it contained appeared to require. He then took a pen, but his hand trembled so much that he could hardly guide it, and occupied himself for some time in what appeared to be simply scribbling. After a time and when the trembling had ceased, he wrote with more purpose, and addressed a letter to John Rasper, Esq.,—a man who had now and then advanced him money on the security of Frank Lockyer,—called to Perks and bade him take it to the address and wait for an answer.

"Put a ticket on the door, Perks," said Cecil, 'Return in two hours.' Close the outer door after you."

"I shan't be gone half that time, sir," replied Jim. "Say an hour."

"Do as you're ordered," said Cecil, more hastily than he usually spoke.

Jim did as he was requested, and when Cecil heard the sound of the closing door he buried his face in his hands and remained some time leaning his head upon the desk. He then walked from room to room, his features assuming the appearance which they had done in the Park, and the cold sweat-drops falling again as they had fallen before. His eyes were perpetually wandering to the office clock, as though the minutes it recorded were being counted impatiently, or were being measured by no real sense of time but by the throbbing of his own beating heart. That he was suffering intensely from some secret cause no one who had seen him could have doubted; but he was alone, shut in, he and his conscience.

Jim returned within the hour, and when Cecil heard the click of the door-latch he almost staggered to a seat.

"Gentleman kept me waiting near a quarter of an hour, or I should been back afore, sir," said Jim, offering a letter.

"Place it on my desk and then close the door."

Cecil spoke with evident difficulty. It was some moments before he went to the desk, and when he did so he covered the letter with his hand as though to hide it from himself. At last he tore open the envelope and took out the contents—a cheque and a small scrap of paper. Cecil uttered a suppressed scream and again laid his head upon his desk, and so he remained for nearly half an hour as though he were asleep or had swooned.

When he recovered he took the cheque in his hand without looking at it, and walked with it to his banker. Had he come out of a grave he could not have looked more pallid—more death-stricken. He went to the coffee-room of an adjoining tavern and wrote a letter to his mother, saying that he should not return home that night, as he was going a short distance out of town with a friend who had assisted him to surmount his difficulties. He had been able to meet his mother when their ruin appeared to be imminent, but now that he had found the means to save them he could not encounter those loving eyes or look upon that sad face—made so sad by undeserved sorrows borne patiently and resignedly.

He then went westward and walked about the streets gazing vacantly into the shop windows, and wondering why he did so. He tried to eat, but his tongue was parched and his lips so feverish that he could not take the food set before him; he drank some champagne—cold, icy cold—and found it pleasant and refreshing. When the evening came on he strolled into the pit of a theatre and sat there until the curtain fell at midnight; but the plots of the different pieces all mingled together in his mind with the events of the morning. His relief from the fear of impending ruin had come so suddenly—so unexpectedly perhaps.

He slept at a tavern, or hotel, or coffee-shop—which he could never remember rightly—and in the morning went to his office, and having drawn a cheque for the amount of the bill due on the following day, received the cash at his banker's and then took a cab to the house of Mr. Skinner. That gentleman had not risen, as he was a late sitter at some house in St. James's—a gambling-house perhaps—and Cecil had to wait in the dining-room until it was Mr. Skinner's pleasure to see him. "Very glad he was to shake hands with Mr. Cecil—very—and hoped that his note had not been misunderstood—was afraid it had been by this anticipatory payment of Mr. Lockyer's bill—punctuality in business was his motter," and so forth. He counted over the crisp bank-notes, and then handed Frank's acceptance to Cecil, remarking:

"Mr. Lockyer writes a fine bold hand, don't he, Mr. Hartley—a good business hand without any flourishes; something very peculiar about his L, though, I should know his L from a thousand."

Why did not Cecil say "yes" or "no," or bid the fellow good-morning before he walked out into the street without waiting for Mr. Skinner's dirty "buttons" to open the door?

"I am right," said Mr. Skinner, peeping over the dirty venetian blinds. "I knew I was. Glad I kept my own counsel. Rasper's done, and I've got my money."

Mr. Skinner hopped up-stairs, two steps at a time, to finish dressing, and hastened to his dressing-room window, which commanded a view of the street down which Cecil was passing.

At first Cecil had nearly run, but now his pace was slow, and ever and anon he stopped and looked back as though a sense of fear possessed him of pursuit or questioning. He could not fly, but must turn like a stag at bay and face his pursuers.

Mr. Skinner rubbing his dirty hands together, resumed his dressing, and during the operation was heard whistling and singing the merriest tunes with which the street bands had made him familiar, so happy was he to think his old friend Phil had been done, and that he himself had got his money.

CHAPTER X.

MR. SKINNER IMPARTS HIS SUSPICIONS TO HIS PARTNER IN THE "BENEVOLENT." — MRS. HARTLEY RETURNS TO HER HUSBAND.

THE ambiguity of Mr. Skinner's observations and conduct at the close of the last chapter may be at once explained.

Mr. Rasper and Mr. Skinner were intimate acquaintances—friends they called themselves, and unkind people called them accomplices — who frequently met at a gaming-house in St. James's, and in whose fortunes they had a pecuniary interest. They found a large portion of "the bank," and the play was conducted on such scientific principles that, whoever might lose, they were not the sufferers. The frequenters of this little Hell were men of position, and none were permitted the *entrée* but by the introduction of some member of a recognised Club; therefore little interruption was feared from the police, and the "Benevolent," as it was called, produced a sure and infamous income to its proprietors. Mr. Skinner was also a book-maker on the turf, and being known in that capacity was permitted intercourse with men who would under any other circumstances have kicked him for speaking to them. Mr. Skinner was suspected of being the "Co." in a firm of advertising quacks bearing a something in excess of a savoury character. Skinner's personal appearance—low brow, large mouth, and a complexion that no saponaceous operation could possibly make clean—did not impress any one in his favour. He was rather "horsy" in his costume, and prodigal of jewellery—real jewellery, amongst which was a diamond brooch blazing in his light-blue stock like a gas-star on an illumination night. He rarely wore gloves, on account of the valuable rings upon his fingers, and those barbaric adornments possibly made the more frequent ablution of his podgy hands inconvenient.

Cecil had been introduced to Mr. Skinner by his necessities, as he had been to Mr. Rasper, and no doubt he deserved the plucking he had met with for resorting to such imprudent and uncommercial means of obtaining money. Cecil was inexperienced and stimulated to make dangerous ventures by strong motives—stronger far than a desire for gain.

The two acquaintances, Mr. Rasper and Mr. Skinner, had met in the small parlour of the "Benevolent," and where they sat usually from ten till two in order to afford temporary accommodation to any of their victims, the profit of those transactions being divided mutually between them, the other partner who superintended the bank having an interest only in the gains of the play. In their private operations each was independent of the other, and their general conversation turned on any successful knavery which had transpired during the day. If Mr. Skinner had picked up a flat at "The Corner" or anywhere else, he expected to be commended for his dexterity by Mr. Rasper; and if Mr. Rasper had made a more than usually good haul in the City, he looked for the congratulations of Mr. Skinner. It was during the interchange of such rascally confidences that Mr. Rasper said:—

"Done a good thing to-day, Skinner—cleared a fifty on a capital three months for £500. Safe as the Bank; did one afore for the same parties, and t'other day the acceptor married a gal with a large fortune."

The amount struck Mr. Skinner as being identical with that of the bill he had been asked to renew in the morning, and so he asked:—

"Who's the parties?"

"Two City men—acceptor a junior in an old-established concern, and the drawer a young chap as is doing very well and has a father that's coining money by buying and selling goods not quite on the square."

"What's their names?" asked Skinner, quite unconcernedly.

Mr. Rasper always liked to be particular on matters of business, and therefore, before he replied, he brought forth his bill-book—Russia leather with a gilt clasp—and took from it a slip of paper which he handed to Skinner, "Them's the parties—Hartley or Lockyer—it's a private transaction between the young men; so was the one I did afore for them."

Mr. Skinner looked at the bill of exchange in his hand as though it were a work of art, and he was anxious to detect its beauties. He was thinking however that Cecil had told him during their brief interview that Mr. Lockyer was abroad, and that he would not return for some days; and yet here was a bill dated yesterday, and accepted by the absentee.

"I think I've heard of Lockyer. Bland and Lockyer's the firm. It ought to be good paper," said Skinner, calmly.

Mr. Skinner did not speak truly to his acquaintance—his old friend Phil Rasper—when he said that; but he consulted his own interest when he returned the bill and said no more on the subject. On the succeeding day he had a similar document to present in due course, and he hoped to get £500 in exchange for it, as he instantly suspected that he should receive the money from which old friend Phil had parted with so much satisfaction. What else Mr. Skinner thought, he kept to himself until he had finished his business with Cecil, and made his commendatory remarks on the caligraphy of Mr. Frank Lockyer.

When Mr. Skinner had finished dressing and eaten an excellent breakfast, he walked leisurely to his banker's and paid in the money he had received from Cecil. Having done this, he paused in the street for a few moments and reflected upon the propriety of calling on his old acquaintance, Phil Rasper, to tell him of certain convictions which had taken possession of him on the preceding evening, and which he had not considered it prudent to communicate to his old friend at the time. After due consideration he resolved to defer the interview until they met in the evening, but wrote a note requesting Rasper to be at the Benevolent half an hour earlier than usual.

Cecil had returned home somewhat before his customary time, and his mother ceased to be surprised at the strange excitement which he exhibited, when she learned that he had, by the unlooked-for aid of a friend, surmounted the difficulty which had appeared so appalling.

He could not eat at dinner, although it was evident he wished to appear happy and at ease, but he took large draughts of water, and his flushed face revealed how feverishly his blood was flowing through his veins. He at all times used wine abstemiously, but now he thrust the decanter from him as though it contained some dreaded poison—some draught which might make him mad enough to utter his hidden thoughts; and he knew what a secret he had taken to himself that day.

We know it also—knew it before Mr. Skinner and Mr. Rasper met at "the Benevolent."

"Oh, I say, Rasper," said Mr. Skinner, "I've been wanting to see you all day; I've been thinking all night through about you and that little bill of Lockyer's which you showed me."

"What about it?" asked Mr. Rasper, calmly.

"I thought I knowed the name of the acceptor, and I remembered after I left you that I once had a bill of his drawn by the same party as yours is—and——"

"Well, it was regular, wasn't it?" asked Rasper with a smile, suspecting his friend of a little professional jealousy.

"Oh yes, *mine* was perfectly regular—paid to the day," replied Skinner; "and perhaps yours will turn out to be all right, but——"

"But what?" asked Rasper, with much animation.

"Mind, I couldn't prove what I'm about to say, and I shouldn't say it at all but to an old friend like you, Phil, because it's no business of mine."

"But it's mine, speak out!" said Rasper, with increased earnestness.

"Well, from what I remember of Mr. Frank Lockyer's signature, I should say you've got a forgery!"

"A forgery!" exclaimed Rasper, turning completely livid.

"Mind I've no proof that it is so, but there is something about the L which don't look to be quite correct. Have you got the bill?" asked Skinner, with most irritating coolness.

"Got it, of course I have!" replied Rasper, instantly producing his Russia-leather bill-case, but opening it with some difficulty, as his fingers trembled violently. "Here it is at last, and that L seems to be a good one."

"Phil, you'll excuse an old friend speaking plainly, but for once you've been done, I *do* believe. Now don't agitate yourself—the best of us is liable to mistakes, and I fancy you've made one. You'd better see the drawer and ask him to have the acceptor's name verified. Go quietly to work. If it's a duffer, you can frighten his friends out of the money; but be calm, old boy."

Mr. Skinner spoke like a man who had had losses, and had learned to disregard them.

"To be done!—me to be done!" said Mr. Rasper, rising and walking about the room. "The money's a lump, and I'll have it somehow; but to be done—that's what stings me. However, I'll go to the drawer's lodgings at once. I've got his private address from the porter, and I'll know how matters stand, or I shan't sleep a wink. He can't be offended at my coming at this time of night asking the question, and if he is I don't care."

The cab conveying Mr. Rasper was soon heard to drive up to the door of Cecil's lodgings. Cecil paused in some observation he was making, and held his breath, his heart beating rapidly. There was a sharp knock at the street-door. It was opened and closed again, and Cecil sat with compressed lips and dilated eyes, listening. The servant of the house opened the door of the room where he was sitting, and then announced "a gentleman," but before she could declare the name, Mr. Rasper entered the room, saying, "Good evening, Mr. Hartley." Cecil knew his man,—he merely bowed to him; and then watched the servant until she had closed the door after her.

Mrs. Hartley's life had been made up of painful surprises, and she saw at a glance that they had not ended when she came under the roof of Cecil.

"You may, or you may not, be surprised at this late visit, Mr. Hartley," began Rasper—but before he could say more Cecil rose up, his face perfectly colourless.

"Come into another room, sir," he said in a hoarse whisper.

"That lady's a relative, I suppose?" asked Rasper.

"Yes, my mother," answered Cecil, moving towards the door.

Rasper instantly concluded that his purpose would be better served by remaining where he was, and so he said—

"Then there's no occasion for concealment, and I would rather say what I have to say here,"—and he seated himself to show his determination to remain.

Cecil was about to remonstrate, when Mrs. Hartley said, "Let me hear what this visit means. Pray go on, sir."

"Very well," replied Rasper. "Yesterday, Mr. Hartley, I gave you the money for a bill for £500 on Mr. Frank Lockyer. Now I've reason to think that there's something wrong about it."

"Pray come with me," Cecil again urged; but Rasper, nearly convinced that Skinner's suspicion was correct, answered doggedly—

"No, sir, I do not move from here until I know the truth. Is that bill forged?"

Mrs. Hartley uttered a sharp scream, and rose from her seat; the cry and action seemed to paralyse Cecil.

"It is so. I see it is!" said Rasper springing up; "and you have done me out of my money!"

"Impossible—it cannot be possible!" cried Mrs. Hartley, going to her son.

"Can't it! but it is, ma'am, as sure as we are here. Look at his guilty face. He doesn't deny it, the scoundrel!"

There was silence for a few moments.

"Now what's to be done?" asked Rasper. "Where's the money? Gone! All of it?"

No answer.

"You're a precious rascal, Mr. Hartley, to rob me and my children in this way. But I'm not to be done so easily; and as I am a living man, unless that money is paid back to me by to-morrow morning, I'll have you up to the Mansion House."

"Is this true, Cecil? Does this man speak

truly?" asked Mrs. Hartley, clenching her hands and holding them up imploringly.

Cecil bowed his head and remained silent.

"You see it is, ma'am. You see he can't deny that he has robbed me. If he don't refund every shilling by to-morrow, I will do what I say."

"To-morrow morning?" asked Mrs. Hartley.

"Yes, and I don't leave this place to-night. I won't lose sight of him, mind that!" replied Rasper.

Mrs. Hartley remained absorbed in thought for a few moments, and then she said—

"You will do nothing, sir, until I return? I may be an hour—perhaps longer."

"I'll not leave this house without my money, however long it may be, or that fellow goes with me in charge of the police," said Rasper emphatically.

Without looking at Cecil again, Mrs. Hartley went to an inner room, and in a few minutes the street door was heard to close, as she went out into the street. When she reached a cab stand she entered one of the vehicles, and ordered the driver to proceed to Suburban Square.

Mr. Selwyn Hartley was in his first sleep when he was awakened by a loud knocking at his door, and before it could have been possible for the servant to have arisen and gone down-stairs, the knocking was repeated. Mr. Hartley's first conjecture was that there were thieves in the house —then that his place in the City was on fire, but no thought of wife or children entered his head.

He jumped out of bed, and having thrown up the window, bawled out to know the cause of the disturbance.

"It is I, Selwyn—your wife—I want to see you instantly," said Mrs. Hartley.

"Oh!" replied Hartley, as he retired from the window much perplexed and greatly vexed at this untimely visit. Having dressed himself partially, he went down-stairs and found his wife sitting once more in her accustomed place, weeping bitterly.

"What's up now, Rebecca?" he asked. "Pray leave off snivelling at that rate, and let me hear what's the matter."

Mrs. Hartley instantly dried her eyes, and after one or two efforts to speak, succeeded at last in a broken voice and the briefest words in telling him the story of Cecil's delinquency.

"Forgery, is it?" said Hartley, when she had ended. "Well, that's more than I expected even from him, a conceited unprincipled puppy! Well, what has brought you here?"

"What has brought me here?" repeated Mrs. Hartley, starting up. "Have I not told you? Have I not told you that the man from whom Cecil had the money is waiting at the house, and will not go until he is repaid?"

"And if he is not repaid?" asked Hartley.

"If he is not?—what do you mean? He will——" The poor mother could say no more.

"He will send for a policeman—that's the usual course, I believe," said Hartley.

"Yes, he said so, but not if he has his money. Give it me, Selwyn! Give it me and let me free Cecil from this danger—this remorse——"

"Me?" exclaimed Hartley. "Me give you £500 to compromise the felony which this bad fellow has committed! As I told you but lately, my money was too dirty for my gentleman's handling—and I now tell you it's too clean to buy him out of a prison."

"Surely I do not understand you? Surely you do not hesitate to save our son——"

"Our son,—your son perhaps, madam," said Hartley fiercely. "He has disowned me long ago. Here in this room he called me a dishonest man—turned up his fine nose at my line of business."

"You will not remember anything that has passed now, Selwyn!" cried Mrs. Hartley. "You will not think of that now that Cecil is in danger of being arrested on such a dreadful accusation?"

"Not remember it? If I were on my death bed and he knelt beside it I would not forgive him—not help him if raising a finger would do it."

"I'll not believe you—I'll not believe you have such a heart of stone!" sobbed Mrs. Hartley.

"You ought to believe what I say, you have had your own experience of my firmness. No, let him go to the friends he has preferred to me—to old Wycherly, who has never tired of traducing me even to my own wife and son, and for whom they both turned their backs upon me and left me to shift for myself as I best could. Where's Mrs. Masham? She's got plenty. She could set son against father; now let her take my place and help him."

"Selwyn, this is unnatural cruelty!" said Mrs. Hartley. "I will not believe that you mean what you say. You only speak such bitter words to give me pain. Admit that Cecil has done all that you say—he is your son—your only living son, and you will not, dare not for your own credit's sake, allow this terrible matter to go on."

"Dare not?" asked Hartley. "Why? What

harm can it do to me? Wife and son, friends and foes have not hesitated to call me a rogue almost to my face, and yet I have prospered in spite of them. What harm can it do me to have it said I am the father of a forger? You and the rest of you have almost called me one, and I have lived it down—made money—can walk the City with my hands in my pocket and look the world in the face, as I've said a hundred times—Dare not!"

"God forgive you for what you have said, Selwyn! I have never spoken one unwifely word concerning you to friend or foe. You must feel that you are the father of this unhappy boy."

"No, a hundred times no!" cried Hartley. "I have striven to do my duty—to feed, clothe and school the children whilst they lived, and to bury them decently when they died, and a precious return I have met with. This undutiful cub is reaping the reward of his treatment of me—the father he's told to honour. He cut me—clean away from him, and now he may get out of the mess he is in as he best can."

"Again I say I will not believe you mean to act thus wickedly, cruelly, unnaturally. Will you see this man? Will you hear what he has to say in the morning?"

"Yes—I don't mind if you wish it, and won't believe what I say now," said Hartley coolly.

"Where shall he come to you, Selwyn? To your office?"

"Yes, anywhere. Come, you're keeping that cab waiting, and it's near twelve o'clock."

Mrs. Hartley believed that in the morning he would stand between his son and the consequences of his crime, and the mother's thankfulness rising in her heart obliterating all her own wrongs and sorrows, she placed her arms around her husband's neck as though they had never been estranged, and kissed him.

"Very well then, good night," said Hartley, returning the salute. "You'll excuse me coming to the door, as I'm afraid of catching cold—and here's half-a-crown for the cab fare."

Mr. Hartley returned leisurely to bed, but despite his selfish stoicism he slept uneasily until it was time to rise.

Meanwhile Cecil and his debtor sat together silently for some time—nearly an hour. Mr. Rasper was the first to speak.

"Mr. Hartley, this is very dull work, and very unprofitable to both on us. Let us have a cigar and talk matters over like men of business, and see what can be done. Try one of these."

Cecil took the proffered cigar, but he did not attempt to light it.

"You have done a very foolish thing," continued Mr. Rasper; "very foolish thing, and many men standing in my shoes would have had you up without giving you a chance of escape. That's not my way. Money before revenge; that's my motto. You've got friends, of course you have—here's your mother, she's got a settlement or annuity, I suppose?"

"Neither; she is entirely dependent on my father," answered Cecil sadly.

"Very well; that's the same sort of thing. Now your father's a rich man?"

"I believe so," replied Cecil.

"Very well then. You've only to let him know what a very foolish thing you've done, and he'll take the bill out of my hands."

Cecil shook his head.

"Not if he knows you're in for transportation? Oh, don't tell me! Fathers has flinty hearts they say, but none on 'em like to have their children lagged, Mr. Hartley, if the money can get 'em off; and here, in your case, it's only a matter of pounds, shillings, and pence."

"I imagine," Cecil said, "that my poor mother has gone to him; if so, we shall soon know his decision, for a cab has stopped at the door."

Cecil rose with the intention of meeting his mother. Mr. Rasper rose also, saying—

"I think you had better let the servant open the door."

Cecil understood what was intended by that observation, and colouring deeply resumed his chair.

Mrs. Hartley came into the room with a faint smile upon her wan face, which Cecil and Rasper both construed into the harbinger of good tidings.

"Well, ma'am, our difficulty's over, I hope?" said Rasper. "If so, I am very glad that I came here without lodging an information."

"I hope the difficulty will be over," replied Mrs. Hartley.

"*Will?*—then you haven't the money?" asked Rasper anxiously.

"No, sir. It was too late to-night for Mr. Hartley—this gentleman's father—to come on to-night; but if you will meet him to-morrow at his office in the City, at one o'clock, he will see you."

"And pay me?" asked Rasper.

"I presume so," replied Mrs. Hartley. "I was not told what to say to you; only to request you to meet my husband in the morning."

"It would have been more satisfactory to have had the money," said Rasper thoughtfully; "but I suppose you told him all the facts of the case, and that I shall take the usual course if the money isn't forthcoming?"

"I told him that, sir, and more," replied Mrs. Hartley

"Very well then. I don't see that I shall do any good by staying here any longer. What is Mr. Hartley's, sen., City address?"

Cecil mentioned it, and Rasper wrote it down on a piece of paper.

"One o'clock; I'll be punctual; and I hope for all our sakes there'll be no hitch in the business. I don't want to lose my money; you don't want to lose your character; and as for hushing such a matter up on account of public morality—why private folks have nothing to do with public morality, as I know on."

With this rather ambiguous observation Mr. Rasper shook hands with Mrs. Hartley first, and then with Cecil, and took his departure.

How the remaining hours of that wretched night were passed by Cecil and his mother, was remembered by both of them throughout their lives.

CHAPTER XI.

MR. SELWYN HARTLEY TAKES COUNSEL WITH HIS ONLY "FRIEND AND PARTNER," AND DETERMINES TO BECOME A COMMERCIAL BRUTUS.—CECIL GOES ANOTHER STAGE ON THE ROAD TO RUIN.

DURING the remaining hours of the night, Mr. Selwyn Hartley (as we have seen) slept uneasily; the crime of his son and its probable consequences would intrude themselves upon his consideration, and generally, as they were likely to affect himself. He and his partner had assiduously made known to such City connections as they had, that Cecil had been discarded, not penniless, certainly, as his father had displayed a munificence towards his offending son, which told as greatly for his parental considera tion as for the abundance of his means. Mr. Selwyn Hartley was therefore blameless, none could accuse him of parsimony or evil counsel, and whatever shame or discredit could attach to Cecil's intimates, must be divided between the Lockyers and the Wycherlys, who had countenanced his disobedience to his father's will, and produced their estrangement. Indeed, he thought that his refusal to conceal the flagrant delinquency of which Cecil had been guilty, would entitle him to be considered a commercial Brutus, who had smothered his personal feelings from a high sense of justice to the trading community—and perhaps induce men to forget what had been spoken to his own discredit. Yes, Cecil was his son, but in name only, as he had repudiated the means whereby he lived, and figuratively spit upon the gaberdine he wore when on the Rialto. It was only thus that he considered Cecil's claim of kindred, for his children had no place in his heart, nor had he any of those loving recollections of infantine endearments which plead so loudly oftentimes in after years on behalf of the prodigal and the erring. Nor had he any sympathy with his patient enduring wife, for whom he had never known that love which had its mysterious birth in heaven, and which purifies the hearts it truly joins together of selfishness in all things. She had been to him the drudge that kept his house and economised his substance—nothing more. She had been dismissed by cruel words, because the powerful love which belongs to her woman's nature could not be stifled in her heart, but would cry out for justice to her children.

No wonder that the voice of self prevailed, when neither wife, nor child, nor worldly interest could be heard in favour of the offender, or that Selwyn Hartley smiled and showed his fine teeth as usual when he gave his morning greeting to his two unscrupulous partners in the City, and afterwards asked their friendly counsel on the course he should pursue, with as much indifference as he would have discussed the value of a job lot, or the probability of another man's bankruptcy.

What the result of the conference of Hartley, Bosbury, Jones, & Co., we shall learn presently.

When Mr. Rasper returned to the "Benevolent," and communicated what had passed to his old friend Skinner, that clever fellow, now sincerely interested in the welfare of his coadjutor, said—

"It's a bad job, but certainly not thorough bad, if you mind how you play your cards. It's a pity there's a family difference, but no man likes to have his son convicted of forgery. You must put the screw on old Hartley in the morning, and frighten him a bit. If I was you, I'd take a friend with me—somebody as would look in the police—do you understand?"

"Yes, certainly," replied Rasper, "and I think your advice is the thing. I know the man to do it, he is in the police, and I once used him to do something of the same sort and got my money."

"Try him again. Police is an excellent institution—sometimes," said Skinner.

"I'll do it in the morning," replied Rasper, as their conversation was interrupted by some requirements of the "Benevolent," with which we have happily no concern.

With downcast eyes and heavy step, his mind oppressed by torturing thoughts, Cecil walked to the City, his little office seeming now the cell of a prison, and every sound a call to judgment. Would his father, forgetting all that name implied, abandon him to the consequences of his crime? Would he whose blood flowed in his veins and who had given him life, be so unmindful of such inseparable ties and cast him into the abyss which yawned at his feet, nor fear to be dragged down with him? Would he who had sworn to cherish her who was his wife unto her life's end, drive home the iron which her son had thrust into her heart? Oh, what was depending on that one man's will—that one man's word!—honour, love, and life, which had been staked so desperately upon a single cast! The thought was maddening, and he pressed his clenched hands upon his forehead to ease the throbbing of his brain. When he became calmer he thought that he would go away, he had money enough for that. Where could he go and leave his crime behind him? A hue and cry would follow him wherever he fled, calling aloud, "Cecil Hartley the forger!" Whose ears would hear it then? Whose eyes would read it on the walls? Might not the sound deafen, the sight blind the dear devoted mother who loved him so tenderly and who had borne so much for his sake? No; better to remain and face the worst. Was it a crime which he had committed, he asked himself? He had intended no wrong to any. He had yielded to a terrible temptation to save others and himself, but was that a crime? Should he proclaim himself a guilty man when his own conscience acquitted him of any evil intention? Better, far better, to declare his innocence by telling all the truth and trust to an even-handed justice for his acquittal.

This comforting delusion would not remain. He had violated the law—he had done that which men, in regard for their common safety, had decreed to be a crime, treacherous and base, and for which they would not long ago have hunted down the trespasser to the foot of the gallows. If his father abandoned him he was lost!—utterly lost!

Eleven o'clock! Two hours more must pass before he could know his fate. Who measures life by time? Neither the very happy nor the very wretched. The golden mean is known to few.

We would not willingly have called in the assistance of the police, knowing how unpopular that prosaic body has become with critics and readers, but as faithful chroniclers we are compelled to retain Mr. Sergeant Tracer just after his receipt of a note from Mr. Rasper, inviting him to call on very particular private business before eleven o'clock.

Sergeant Tracer closed his eyes for a few moments when he had read the note and appeared to be meditating the acceptance or the rejection of Mr. Rasper's invitation, and having made up his mind, he took down his hat from its appointed peg and went out of the station-house.

Mr. Rasper had just finished breakfast when Tracer was announced, and as bottled beer had formed one of the items of that early meal the policeman was invited to take a glass before commencing business.

Sergeant Tracer declined with rather a curt, "No, thank'ee, sir."

"Very well; then to business," said Mr. Rasper. "I have sent for you, Sergeant, as a man in whom I have the greatest confidence and to put a £10 note in your pocket."

"Much obliged, sir."

"I have, I am sorry to say, been done—done in a very shabby way, and to some amount."

Mr. Rasper paused for an observation, but receiving none went on—

"I have reason to believe—in fact to know—that I have cashed a forged bill for a young party, and I am anxious to get my money back again."

"Indeed, sir!" said Tracer quietly.

"Yes, and I think I can manage it with a little of your private assistance; private, you know, because a fuss won't do it," observed Rasper.

"Who's the party, sir?" asked Tracer.

"A young chap in the City. His father is a rich man, and I want you to go with me and remain in sight whilst I have an interview with the father. You will make the matter look in earnest, and I've no doubt he'll take up the difficulty out of my hands. For this job I'll give you £10."

Tracer bowed, and said, "Have you got the bill about you, sir?"

"I have," replied Rasper, producing his Russia bill-book and then the bill. "There it is, Hartley, or Lockyer—Lockyer's the forgery, and I've been done.'

"Well, sir," said Tracer, "my course of duty's very clear,"—folding up the bill and retaining it —"I have only to take the party into custody and you can appear against him."

There were three conclusive reasons with Mr

Tracer why he decided upon this unexpected course of action.

1st. Mr. Rasper, upon the former occasion of employing Mr. Tracer, to which he had referred, formed a very inadequate estimate of the Sergeant's services, and could not be made to reconsider his valuation.

2nd. Mr. Hartley, sen., had given Mr. Tracer a great deal of unprofitable trouble by the clever way in which he transacted his business, always evading the law when it seemed on the point of catching him.

3rd. Sergeant Tracer was anxious for promotion, and he believed that the next important case which came into his hands would probably lead to an inspectorship.

For the above reasons he had astonished Mr. Rasper by the statement of what he considered to be his duty.

"Take the party into custody! I don't want that. I could have had that done without you; I want to get my money back."

Rasper saw the mistake he had made and being a quick man at figures instantly determined that he had better lose twenty pounds than five hundred, and having, moreover, an unlimited belief in the influence of money, he smiled blandly at Tracer and said—

"Of course you will do your duty—your duty to yourself, and I'll be plain at once. Help me in this business and I'll give you twenty pounds."

That was a large sum for Tracer to weigh against three and twenty shillings a week and his duty.

"You've mentioned this affair to a friend or two, I suppose?" asked Tracer.

"Yes, to one Mr. Skinner, of the 'Benevolent,'" replied Rasper.

"Mr. Skinner—oh yes—I know the party—and to—who else?"

"To Hartley and a lady——"

"A lady and Hartley," said Tracer quickly, as the case appeared to have a chance of slipping through his fingers. "Well, sir, unless in the interest of the public you intend——"

Mr. Rasper expressed his value of the public very emphatically.

"Very well, sir," said Tracer. "Then I should advise you to lose no time, in case some party should talk, and secrecy be impossible. Let's go to the young man's father—and he's a sharp one."

Mr. Rasper acceded to this proposal and went at once to Mr. Hartley's office, arriving there shortly after the partners had concluded their discussion which decided the fate of Cecil.

Mr. Rasper and his attendant Tracer were instantly received by Mr. Hartley and Mr. Bosbury with as much cool ceremony as though they had come upon some ordinary commercial business, and not, as both knew, on a matter affecting the honour—the future life of Cecil.

"I wish to speak to you alone, sir," said Rasper, rather bothered by the formality of their reception.

"I have no secrets from this gentleman, my partner, Mr. Bosbury," said Hartley.

"Well, sir, then—" Mr. Rasper was really confused—"I have come about that unpleasant matter of your son—and this is Sergeant Tracer."

"If that is your business," replied Hartley, "I have already told Mr. Bosbury my determination, my—unalter—able determination, and which he will communicate to you at once. Good morning." Mr. Hartley showed his white teeth, bowed, and left the room.

Mr. Rasper augured very unfavourably from this peculiar conduct of Mr. Hartley, but being a man of the world he concluded, after a few minutes' thought, that this was only the prelude to an offer of compromise in some form or the other.

He was never more mistaken in the course of his long and tricky life.

Mr. Bosbury had listened in perfect silence to Mr. Hartley's statement, being anxious to ascertain whether his principal inclined to mercy or to justice; and finding that the commercial Brutus had no intention of saving his unhappy son, coincided in that view as the only one which could be fairly taken by a British merchant, the more especially as it would effectually remove Cecil from any future interference in his father's affairs, and smooth the way to a further advancement of Mr. Bosbury.

"Now, sir," said Rasper, "please begin."

"My task is painful and short," replied Mr. Bosbury. "We have gone fully into this matter, and considered the *pros* and *cons* of the case, and have determined not to interfere, but allow Mr. Cecil Hartley to clear out of this business as well as he can."

"But do you understand what it is?" asked Rasper, astounded. "It's forgery—transportation."

"So Mr. Hartley understood," said Bosbury, calmly, "and therefore, upon public grounds alone, Mr. Hartley, as a member of the great commercial community of this city, declines to interfere."

"And the young man his own son—his own flesh and blood?" asked Rasper, amazed more than ever. "If he hadn't got the money—if he couldn't pay—I should have——"

"He has the money, and could pay, replied Bosbury; "but this is a matter of principle, and where that is concerned Mr. Hartley is a Queen Anne's statue, sir—rock—perfect rock."

"Good morning, sir," said Tracer, who had hitherto kept silence. "We'd better go, Mr. Rasper—you'll get nothing by staying here:" adding in a whisper as they passed through the warehouse, "You may get your money when they find you're in earnest—and you may not."

When Mr. Rasper walked out again into the street, he was very red in the face, whilst the officer appeared to be perfectly unmoved, and prepared for either fortune—the twenty pounds or the case.

"Well, I couldn't have believed it of any man," said Rasper, "not even of a Hottentot! Not save his only son!"

"I never knew but one other like him in my experience," replied Tracer. "Well—now you'll let things take their course?"

"Certainly!" replied Rasper. "He may dub up as I said if he finds us in earnest."

An hour afterwards Sergeant Tracer and Mr. Rasper were seen to leave the Mansion House together, and proceed direct to the office of Cecil Hartley. Jim Perks opened the door, and showed them into Cecil's room. He stood as though expecting them, calm—quite calm—and his face as rigid and cold as stone. Few words passed between them.

"Call a four-wheeled cab, young man," said Tracer, and Perks obeyed, soon returning with the required vehicle.

"Perks," said Cecil in a low, hollow voice, "go—go to my mother—tell her—tell her all is over. You will find her I think at my father's—in the City."

He then walked out into the street, followed closely by Tracer and Rasper, and getting into the cab, the officer called to the driver, "Mansion House, side door," and the words almost stunned Cecil as he heard them.

Poor Jim Perks, from his own sad experience, guessed the truth near enough to make him run at his utmost speed on his miserable errand, losing in his astonishment and distress all recollection of Hartley and their former relation, and intent only on breaking his mournful news as gently as he could devise to the kind lady who had helped him when fresh from prison, and when she little foreboded that the poor gaol-bird would come to her the bearer of such tidings of her son.

Breathless almost, Jim rushed into the warehouse, and with difficulty requested to see Mrs. Hartley, if she were there.

"What's your name?" asked the man he had addressed.

"Oh, never mind my name," replied Jim; "say Mr. Cecil's porter."

The message was delivered; and Mrs. Hartley instantly left the room, or counting-house, where she had been pleading for her son, and recognising Jim Perks, even in the gloom of the warehouse, went to him.

"Well?" She could say no more.

"Don't look so scared, ma'am," answered Jim, "or I shall be afeard to speak, and I've bad news to tell."

"What?"

"Muster Cecil has gone away with two—two friends, perhaps; and he tould me to find you, ma'am, and say that 'all was over.'"

Mrs. Hartley uttered a shrill scream, and swooned, falling into the arms of Jim Perks, who, without waiting to be directed, carried her to the room she had just left, pushing aside, as he did so, Mr. Hartley, who had been roused by the sound of his wife's voice.

"It's killed her!—It's killed her!" said Jim, placing Mrs. Hartley in a chair.

"What's killed her, you fool?" asked Hartley, looking rather anxiously at his wife's pale face.

"The bad news I've brought her of your son,

Mr. Hartley," replied Jim. "You'd better send for a doctor, I'm thinking."

"You're thinking!" said Hartley, recognising the speaker. "You'd better take yourself off, I'm thinking, unless you want to be turned out."

"At your peril, Mr. Jacob Hartley!" answered Jim. "Lay a finger on me and I'll make you sorry for it. I won't go until I see this good lady tended, as my master's got trouble enough on his hands, I know, to have any doubt of his mother joined to it."

Assistance had been given to Mrs. Hartley by people about the place, and she presently recovered her consciousness. When she recognised Jim Perks she stared wildly for a few minutes, and then said—

"Is it too late? Is it indeed too late?"

"I told my message, ma'am,' replied Jim; "and you know best what it meaned. He went away in a cab with a man and another."

"Selwyn, do you hear what this man says?"

asked Mrs. Hartley. "Did you hear what he said to me, 'All is over'?"

"I've heard a deuced lot of nonsense this morning," replied Hartley.

"You will remember what you have heard at the most solemn hour of your life, if consciousness is left you—wicked man! You cannot die with those words unremembered. You have destroyed your son—blasted his life—broken his heart, as you have broken mine. You could have saved all this misery by giving what you only value for your selfish enjoyment. You have sent our child to prison—to shame—to death, I hope, for then we shall be the sooner together."

"I have done what is right to myself and to society, ma'am," said Hartley. "I have let an undutiful, ungrateful son—as this fellow's presence proves—reap the reward of his own wilfulness. I appeal to these gentlemen if I haven't. I have done my duty to the commercial interest by not standing between a forger and his just punishment. I appeal to these gentlemen if I haven't."

"*You* talk of forging!" cried Jim Perks, confronting Hartley. "You say that and me standing by! There can be no harm in breaking the wicked oath I took——"

But Jim's intended revelation was prevented by the entrance of three or four stout fellows from the warehouse, who had been summoned by Mr. Bosbury at a sign from Mr. Hartley.

"Let the man wait for me—let him," said Mrs. Hartley. "I know not what is to become of me—what I shall have to do. Let me have some one who has a human heart in his breast—and there is no other here!"

"Thank you for self and partners," said Mr. Hartley; "and now, perhaps, as there's nothing more to be said or done at present, and as business has to be attended to, perhaps you had better go to your lodgings and take that fellow off my premises."

Mrs. Hartley made no reply, but rose up calmly; and after adjusting her dress as though she were conscious of all that she was doing, left the counting-house and passed into the street, followed by Perks. She then appeared bewildered, and looked about her uncertain which way to go, until Perks spoke to her and advised that he should call a cab and take her home.

"Yes—home," she said. "Cecil will not be there, I presume?"

"Not just now, I fancy, ma'am," answered Jim; "but I'll go to him by-and-by, and let you know when he's coming."

With this assurance, Mrs. Hartley appeared to be perfectly content, and then, with Jim on the box, allowed herself to be driven to her lodging. Let us respect her sorrow and leave her to her tears and to her prayers.

Perks found the little office in charge of a policeman, who was examining the papers in Cecil's desk, and making himself master of the situation; curtly informing Jim that he could remain or go as best suited his convenience. From this man Perks learned what had taken place at the Mansion House—that Mr. Bland,

Frank's partner, had disclaimed the signature upon the bill as that of Mr. Lockyer—that Cecil, having remained perfectly silent, had been remanded to Newgate until such time as Frank returned and completed the evidence against his friend.

Jim Perks at once resolved to go to his unhappy master, taking with him a letter brought by the foreign post, and which he had received unknown to the policeman, who might otherwise have considered it part of the case and detained it.

Cecil Hartley was in prison.

What varying significations that word prison has! A prison to the houseless, foodless wretch sounds oftentimes like the name of a blessed refuge, where sleep is to be enjoyed and hunger is to be satisfied. To the hardened, dissolute rogue a prison means restraint from his coarse debaucheries and compulsion to labour for his daily dole—a lot which he abhors, although his predatory life is full of terrors which drive him to seek oblivion in sensuality and drunken riot. To such as Cecil, gently nurtured, early taught to respect honour and virtue as the charms of life—to fear shame more than the chance of death—to know that to have the prison taint upon one, is to become infected with a moral leprosy which makes men turn away their eyes and shun you, to try even true love to its uttermost, and to make old friendship forgetful of its early protestations. What are the rough walls and cross-barred windows which make a prison? They are as a tomb wherein the better part of life is buried, with few to mourn, and fewer still to pity or excuse.

By the graciousness of a kind governor, Jim was permitted to see his master—see him through iron bars—and to have conveyed to him the letter he had brought. Cecil charged the poor fellow with some brief message for his mother, and his promise to write to her in the morning; and then they were parted.

The letter was from Frank, and dated Genoa—a word of pleasant sound.

Much cheerful gossip of travel and new scenes,

new hopes, and a few old recollections, and kindly anticipations of the time when they should meet again, was succeeded by a few of the saddest and most distressing lines Cecil had ever read, though he who penned them believed that they would have been the most welcome that he could have written to his friend.

"And now to prove traitor to my pretty, gentle wife, and all to give pleasure to my dear old friend, who has always mistrusted his own worth and fascinations. Do you remember a little purple diary which Ruth kept under lock and key, and in which she was wont to make a daily chronicle of the important nothings of her life? Of course you remember it. Well, old boy, you and I little thought we were the heroes of that romance. By much coaxing, and more marital cruelty, I obtained a peep into that volume, swearing upon Ruth's lips never to divulge what I should read until the proper time. 'At lovers' perjuries Jove laughs,' and at husbands' also, let us hope, for I am about to forget my vows, unless, as I believe, the proper time has come to tell the secret.

"In that little book there is set down many a record of F. L. and his sayings and doings; but that might be conjectured, seeing what has happened; but who would have thought that 'Cousin C. said this, and Cousin C. said that,' fill many a page? For whose perusal, think you? Not my Ruth. No; she loved me from the first. No; not my Ruth. Who then? If you cannot answer this question yourself, then you wrote me untruly when you said that you loved Kate Wycherly."

A mist came between Cecil's eyes and the paper which he read. A mist, a darkness, hot tears, and utter wretchedness.

Such a letter at such a time! Such promises of unimagined happiness at such a season of hopeless misery! Lost! all lost! and by the act which he had hoped would have obtained the most coveted desires of his life. Kate had loved him, or at least had regarded him with a gracious interest that might have grown into love and made him as dear to her as Frank had been to Ruth.

Lost now—quite lost! She would never hear his name but his dishonour would be remembered with it. Like father, like son! and she would in time believe that he had been undeserving of her regard, and perhaps despise herself for having found a place in her thoughts for one so utterly unworthy as he—the forger!

The lights are lowered, the warder turns the key in the great lock, and Cecil Hartley feels that he is in prison.

CHAPTER XII.

MR. SELWYN HARTLEY SHOWS HIS SYMPATHY WITH CECIL.—FRANK PROVES HIS FRIENDSHIP, AND CECIL IS SELF-CONDEMNED.

"THIS is a very sad affair, sir," said Mr. Bosbury, when his principal, Mr. Hartley, came to business on the following morning. "The case is reported at some length. Would you like to see it, sir?" and Mr. Bosbury handed the newspaper.

"I think not," replied Hartley. "It is not a pleasant thing to see your son's name under the head of Mansion House, and accused of forgery, Mr. Bosbury."

"Dear me, sir, I had no idea after our conversation yesterday that you cared to have prevented such an exposure," said Mr. Bosbury.

"Well, I didn't think I should have felt it so

much, considering the course of conduct Master Cecil has adopted towards me; but I met Croupard—Croupard & Goss—just now, and I find that I am the victim of misconstruction, if not of misrepresentation," replied Hartley.

"How so, sir?" asked Bosbury.

"Why my—my consideration for the commercial interests of this great community, as I may call the City, seems to be—well, seems to be—unlikely to meet its just reward; and when I offered my hand to Croupard, he—he—well, he didn't take it, but made use of such an offensive expression that I can't repeat it to you, Bosbury—to you who know me so well."

"Oh! you mustn't attribute Croupard's conduct to the Mansion House affair," said Bosbury, cheerily. "Recollect they were creditors of that fellow we bought——"

"Oh! to be sure," replied Hartley, "that's it, I shouldn't wonder. Croupard ought to be ashamed of himself to bear malice. He's a bad lot, Mr. B.—a bad lot. Let's have a glass of sherry."

Mr. Hartley knew better than to accept Mr. Bosbury's consolatory suggestion; but he did not care to continue the subject.

The only further notice that Mr. Selwyn Hartley took of his unhappy son's position at present was to the following effect :—

MANSION HOUSE.

TO THE EDITOR OF ——.

SIR,—

As some misapprehension appears to exist in quarters likely to be prejudicial to our interests, will you oblige us by allowing us to state that Mr. Cecil Hartley, charged yesterday at the Mansion House with forgery, has no business connection whatever with our firm.

SELWYN HARTLEY, BOSBURY,
JONES, & CO.

The commercial Brutus could do no less than make this declaration, and as certainly he could do no more to publish the delinquency of Cecil.

Mr. Wycherly, his daughter Kate, and Mrs. Masham were on their way home, resting in Paris for a few days. The tour had proved very beneficial to Kate, and all were looking forward with pleasurable anticipations to their return to Old Court.

Mr. Wycherly, like most Englishmen, was a great newsmonger, and accordingly he had become a subscriber for the week to *Galignani's*. He had taken his seat in an easy-chair for his morning's reading, but had scarcely opened the paper when his eye caught Selwyn Hartley & Co.'s letter, which he read with considerable surprise and pain. The paper of the preceding day he had not seen, and probably he would have remained ignorant of the calamity which had befallen Cecil until his return to England, had not the father's letter attracted his attention. To possess himself of further particulars was perfectly natural, and he read with increased regret the charge against Cecil, and his apparent admission of its truth.

Wycherly instantly returned to his hotel, and

found Ruth and Mrs. Masham dressed for a promised drive, and both in the highest spirits.

"Really, papa," said Kate, "you are very good to-day. You are half-an-hour before your appointment. Luckily we are dressed. We shall enjoy ourselves so much."

"I'm afraid not," replied Wycherly, "when you hear what has brought me back, my dear."

"What, papa?" asked Kate, smiling.

"Well; I am sure I shall shock you both very much, and I am so stupid at breaking good or bad news——" He paused.

"Pray speak plainly," said Mrs. Masham; "anything — anything affecting Ruth or her husband?"

"No, nothing; not quite such close connections," replied Wycherly; "but it concerns one whom we all liked and respected, I believe. Cecil Hartley."

Kate became deadly pale, and opened her large eyes as though she would read in her father's face what she had not power to ask.

"What has happened to Cecil?" said Mrs. Masham, earnestly. "Is he ill?"

"Worse," replied Wycherly.

"Not dead, I trust?" said Mrs. Masham.

Kate pressed her lips together until they were bloodless.

"Worse even than that, I should say were he my son."

Wycherly then told them what he had read, and was not surprised—no—he was not surprised when Kate and Mrs. Masham gave way to a passion of tears.

Wycherly knew that they had found their best, their natural relief from this sudden distress, and therefore he did not hesitate to leave them together, whilst he sauntered up and down the Boulevard in front of the hotel.

It was fortunate for Kate, for himself also, that he had been thus considerate, as he would have learned, as Mrs. Masham learned to suspect henceforth, that one pure heart loved the guilty man; that one pure soul poured out in passionate words its prayers for the offender in his distant prison, believing in the innocency of his transgression, and acquitting him of all premeditated wrong.

What cared she for a violated law, for the cruel vengeance of 'society?' Was it not Frank Lockyer—his friend—his brother, whose name he had written, knowing that there was nothing which that friend would have denied him? She thought and spoke with her whole woman's heart, and reason could not answer her.

This outbreak of her dismay at an end, Mrs. Masham soothed her as women only have the power to soothe each other; and when a calm had come upon Kate's spirit, she told her, in gentlest words, that what had passed should remain between them, and that she should ever have a mother's counsel, as she had already nearly a mother's love.

Kate had now a part to play which would call into action the subtlest art and the most enduring energy. She had to conceal from the searching scrutiny of her father's love, the secret hidden in her heart, to hear of Cecil and give no sign that her pulse quickened at his name, to listen to his dispraise, and speak no word in his defence, but to accede by her silence to what her father affirmed —'that there was truth in blood, as he had said a hundred times, and that son and sire were worthy of each other.' Cruel, cruel words! spoken by any lips, but doubly so when her own dear father uttered them. She would have rejoiced to have hastened home to where Cecil's prison was, and yet she feared to show by word or action that such was the earnest wish of her heart when her father proposed to shorten their stay in Paris, and to affect to be indifferent to all but his good pleasure.

And why? To deceive him? Yes. Had she not led him to believe that he was to have no rival in her love, and he had come to think there could be a place only for him, and to desire that it should be so? He was never to be undeceived so long as his belief made him happier. She had made this compact with him before she knew how hard it would be to keep its conditions.

The first letters which Frank received from home informed him of Cecil's desperate proceeding. The first communication made by his partner Mr. Bland was formal and condemnatory, reminding Frank of the advice which he had rejected, and of the consequences which had been in part foreseen. Frank was astounded at what he read. Another letter was from Cecil. There was no address, only a date, but the painful contents of the letter left no doubt as to the miserable writer's whereabout. It detailed at great length the struggle which Cecil had had with himself, and as it is already recorded, how the temptation grew too strong until he yielded at last, but never believing that he could thereby injure anyone by the act which had made him a felon. He asked no consideration for himself, no friendly succour or sacrifice; all that he appeared to desire in writing that long letter was to satisfy his friend that he had designed no wrong to him, that shameful as his conduct might seem, he was not guilty judged by his own conscience. Nor by Frank. No—he acquitted Cecil of any guilty intention—of any dishonourable thought, and having told Ruth what had occurred, she approved his determination to return to England with the best speed in order that he might at once accept the responsibility of Cecil's obligation.

What a meeting between those long-tried friends! Grim prison bars interposed and repelled the grasp of their hands. The gloom of the prison-house hid almost their faces from each other. The whole wide world was free to one to come and go: to the other there were the limited prison yard and the common prison room, the compelled hours of rising and lying down, and the terrible noise of the warder's key turning in the lock. But Cecil derived great comfort from the visit of Frank, for he heard from the lips of the dear friend he was said to have injured, that he loved and honoured him still, and would stand forward in his defence whenever he found an accuser.

With that assurance Cecil went cheerfully to his hard bed, the words of his friend making such pleasant music, that he slept as though there was no to-morrow, when he was again to endure the humiliation and the shame of being publicly accused of attempting to betray his friend, and to cheat the respectable Mr. Rasper. The painful ordeal was of short duration; and though Frank expressed his undiminished confidence in Cecil's honour and probity, he was told that the place he was in was not the proper one for such a statement. There they only inquired into men's wickedness, and left it to British juries to discover the virtues of the accused.

The sessions were happily near at hand, or the dreadful suspense would have been almost insupportable. When he looked back he was appalled at the folly of the crime he had committed! When he reflected, he saw that the worst consequences which could have proceeded from the first difficulty would have been easily surmounted and retrieved; but now, all that made life valuable had been sacrificed, and pain augmented a hundred-fold to those for whose sake he had committed the rash and criminal act which had destroyed him.

Frank Lockyer in his anxiety to rescue Cecil would have incurred some peril to himself had it been possible to have procured the absence of Rasper; but Sergeant Tracer, having his own promotion in view, had the money-lender placed under heavy recognizances to do his duty to the public and assert the majesty of the law. Mr. Rasper was a very unwilling public benefactor, and would have compounded the felony without one twinge of his patriotic conscience.

What could be done, however, Frank did earnestly, and the most accomplished counsel were retained to plead for a mitigation of punishment, their client's guilt having been in part admitted.

The day of trial came, and when Cecil heard

his name called aloud in the prison-yard, he felt almost relieved by the certainty that the worst would be soon known. He had no hope of escape—none.

Cecil passed through the gloomy passages leading to the court, and stepped into the dock. He cast one hurried look around, and saw in that momentary survey a scene which never left his memory—never; a scene which he could recall at will so long as he lived in all its vividness. The judges on the bench, the counsel at the bar, the jury in the box, the witnesses and idlers in the court, and Frank Lockyer looking up to where the prisoners stood,—all passed in a moment to his brain, and stunned it nearly. Cecil closed his eyes and leaned his head upon his hand, but he could not shut out the scene he had looked upon. He saw it still—clear, distinct, and terrible, and so it continued until he was challenged to plead. He would at once have confessed his guilt, but his legal friends prevailed upon him to say "Not Guilty," in order that should any flaw be discovered why judgment should not be given against him, he might have the benefit of that forlorn hope.

Mr. Rasper gave his evidence briefly and fairly enough.

Mr. Tracer was rather more diffuse, and produced the papers found at Cecil's office, and whereon he had discovered many attempts at imitating the signature of Frank Lockyer.

Other evidence was given by bankers' clerks and James Perks, all tending to criminate the prisoner.

When Frank Lockyer's name was called, poor Cecil was seen to tremble as though an ague had seized him; and when he raised his head to wipe away the cold large drops of sweat upon his face, it was as that of a dead man.

Frank also was greatly agitated, and when asked to admit or deny the authenticity of his signature, he could not speak for some time.

"I wish to make a few observations before I answer the question, gentlemen," Frank said,

"Mr. Hartley and myself have been intimate—most intimate friends from boyhood; indeed we have been as brothers to each other, and I have nothing in the world he has not the right to consider his in part. He knew this; but it was not until I had again and again insisted upon his availing himself of my credit, that he consented to use my name for the honourable advancement of his business. He had a right to do as he has done, and I should have recognised that right at the proper time."

Cecil's counsel looked pointedly at the jury when Frank had made this declaration, and possibly had they been asked for their verdict at that moment Frank's pardonable sophistry might have prevailed, and Cecil received an acquittal. But Justice had to be satisfied.

"Do you say that you authorised the prisoner at the bar to use your signature?" was the next question asked of Frank.

"I say again that our intimacy—our close friendship—gave him the right to believe that I should willingly have acknowledged any responsibility he had required me to accept."

"Is that your handwriting, Mr. Lockyer?" asked the counsel for the Crown.

"Mr. Hartley has admitted, I believe, that it is not," replied Lockyer; "but I am prepared to acknowledge this bill as though it had been made by me, and am willing to pay the money it represents."

"Is that your signature, sir? Yes or No, if you please," repeated the counsel.

Frank paused, and for the first time since he had entered the witness-box ventured to look at Cecil. There was that dear friend—his head bowed down, his face covered to hide his shame, and his whole frame convulsed with the agony which possessed him.

Frank turned his eyes away and looked piteously at the judges.

"Why am I required to make answer, knowing what it implies? I say again, my lord, that Mr. Hartley had a right—a moral right—to use my name in any way he pleased. He knew I should not have refused my consent, and so believing he acted rightly."

"That is not the law, sir," replied the judge. "And you must answer the question. Had the prisoner your legal authority to accept that bill in your name?"

"Do not—do not compel me to answer that question," said Frank, clasping his hands. "He is my dearest friend—my brother. Do not compel me to answer."

"No," cried Cecil looking up, his eyes inflamed and staring, and every line in his face deepened into blackness. "No, you shall not be compelled to answer, dear friend. I had no authority to use his name. I am guilty."

A buzzing murmur spread throughout the Court, and the venerable men upon the bench conferred together, looking kindly towards the poor prisoner at the bar, now erect and regarding them steadfastly to hear his doom pronounced.

When the jury returned, and had given their verdict "Guilty," Cecil's counsel made an eloquent appeal in mitigation of the sentence about to be pronounced, urging the prisoner's youth and inexperience, and above all, by the act of using Lockyer's name, the conviction he must have had that he was doing wrong to no one.

How Mr. Rasper cursed his own precipitancy when he heard all this, and mentally vowed not to give Sergeant Tracer a shilling, as without his advice he should probably have temporised for a few days and recovered his money.

Back again to prison. A condemned man now, Cecil took his place among the wretched outcasts who were to be his fellow-workers for long years to come, and who regarded him as reduced to an equality with themselves—down to the dregs from which they had crawled into existence.

The first morning after his condemnation he was ordered to dress himself in the convict livery, badged and numbered, and to lose the sound of his name, passing as it were, into a new world of misery—misery which would have been unendurable but for the hope that death or freedom would come at some distant day.

Would his dear mother seek to see him in this shameful dress—in this shameful place? The sight would kill her; and yet to part from her without a word, an embrace,—that would kill her also.

They did part without a meeting, as the shock of Cecil's sentence bore her down, and for many weeks she could not leave her room, and then Cecil was gone. Her weakened over-excited brain made her mind confused and wandering, and she never appeared fully to comprehend (happily) the nature of his punishment or the place to which he had been sent, although she knew he was in durance somewhere.

Frank Lockyer came as often as the prison rules permitted him, and Cecil was comforted by this proof that his old true friend did not condemn him as his father had condemned him.

Oh! that cruel father! With jaunty step and smiling face he tried to cheat men of their good opinion; but so unnatural had been his conduct that he was made to feel in a hundred ways that he was to be henceforth an isolated man, though a great city and its million souls were round about him.

One poor fellow would not be kept away from his convict master—Jim Perks; and he, knowing from his own sad experience a prisoner's wants, played his humble part—a servant still.

"You'll soon leave here, sir, the warder tells me," said Jim during one of his visits, "and then, sir, there'll be little or no chance of any friend a seeing you."

"So I believe," replied Cecil sadly.

"You're leavin' good ones to be sorry for you," said Jim; "some as you know and some as you don't, sir. There's one as was speakin' to me the other day and sayin', 'Jim, it's very likely poor Mr. Cecil may have somethin' he wishes done when he's gone—somethin' or other,' this friend says."

"No, Jim," answered Cecil, coldly.

"'Cos if you thought he had,' says the friend, 'and it would give him any comfort to know it was done, you might say it should be seen to, you know.' Do ye see, sir?"

This roundabout speech was difficult of interpretation at first, but Cecil at last fancied it might have some relation to Mr. Garrett's small annuity, and perhaps Mrs. Masham had spoken.

"There is one who will suffer inconvenience I suppose by my misfortune; but I have been so stunned by my own distress that I had forgotten him—Mr. Garrett, poor fellow! However, he must bear as I do."

"On course, sir,—on course," replied Jim; "but if it will comfort you, sir, I shouldn't wonder but other friends will be found for him."

Cecil was, as he had said, so oppressed by his own sorrow that he had little interest left in any other matter, but the poor faded schoolmaster came back to him so touchingly that he said: "Yes, Jim, it would comfort me to know that he was cared for. I wish it were possible." And this kindly remembrance of poor Jerry was like gold put out at usance.

Cecil's transgression was only a nine days' wonder. He passed out of honourable life into convict existence, mourned indeed by the few faithful friends who had truly known and truly loved him; but his place in the great city was soon filled, and his name in a very brief space of time was forgotten, even by Mr. Rasper, as Frank so managed Cecil's affairs that all his just debts were paid.

Poor Cecil!

END OF VOL. II.

CPSIA information can be obtained
at www.ICGtesting.com
Printed in the USA
LVHW040024180422
716440LV00005B/447

9 783752 594287